THE
COLD SPRINGS
KILLER

THE COLD SPRINGS KILLER

M. E. HANSEN

The Cold Springs Killer Copyright © M. E. Hansen, 2022, 2024

All rights reserved. No part of this publication may be reproduced, stored in, or introduced into a retrieval system, or transmitted, in any form, or by any means (electronic, mechanical, photocopying, recording, or otherwise), without the written permission of the copyright owner.

ISBN: 978-1-956167-04-7 Ebook | Kindle Edition
ISBN: 978-1-956167-05-4 | Paperback
Printed in the USA

10 9 8 7 6 5 4 3 2

AUTHOR'S NOTE

This is a work of fiction which contains the following: teen drinking, moderate supernatural gore, and suicide.

Names, characters, places, and incidents are either the product of the author's imagination or are used fictitiously, you'll never really know for sure, unless you chat with the author about it, but for legal reasons any resemblance to actual persons, living or dead, events, or locales is entirely coincidental, so read at your own risk and entertainment.

OTHER WORKS BY M. E. HANSEN

NOVELLAS

Whispers of Addington Manor
The Cold Springs Killer
The Thief's Betrayal

SHORT FICTION

Remembering Emma
The Investigation of Camp Tree Trail
The Greaters and The Lessers
The Problem With Margaret Hennessy
A Deadly Walk Home

To the men in my life who have given
me their support and kindness.
Thanks for the opportunities of growth.

I also dedicate this book to those
who feel alone in their struggles.
You are never alone.
You are loved.
You are needed.
You are enough.

—M. E. Hansen

ONE

atthew Larsen clutched the steering wheel and watched his three friends hoist the metal gate blocking the gravel driveway. Ignoring the bold black letters warning them to keep out of Grover's Pike Campgrounds, they pushed the barrier to the side of the road and high-fived each other.

As he stared at the open space beyond the windshield, Matthew's stomach hardened to lead. They shouldn't have come here. With numerous animal attacks throughout the summer, it wasn't safe. Trespassing at the campground and drinking a case of beer Jason stole from his house could also get the police involved.

Matthew had only agreed to come when Jason had compromised and said they didn't have to spend the night like they usually did. It was tradition to hold a campout the last Friday night of summer break, and they couldn't break it this year. Next week, they would start their senior year of high school, and the heavy reality of this being their final Friday made the night extra special, more important, more final.

Though Jason promised they'd only stay a few hours, Matthew yearned to make a U-turn in the campground and go home, but he'd never hear the end of it from Jason, and stranding his friends was the last thing he wanted to do.

Matthew released the brake, and the cherry red Honda crept over the property line. He stopped and idled as Jason Fink climbed into the passenger seat. The two remaining boys, Kevin Hancock and Rodney Hess, tumbled into the back, laughing and cheering.

"This is going to be the best night ever," Rodney said from the backseat. "Hand me the graham crackers."

Kevin lifted the already opened plastic package of crackers and helped himself before handing them to Rodney.

"You guys, wait two more minutes until we're there," Matthew said as he slowly navigated along the narrow dirt road. "If you leave one crumb, my dad will find it."

Kevin laughed, making a big show of holding his

graham cracker out the open window to keep the car safe from crumbs. "Why did we bring these, anyway? We can't even have a fire without drawing attention, so it's not like we can turn these into s'mores."

Seeing the opportunity, Matthew suggested, "Maybe we should do something else. We could set up a tent in my backyard and watch a movie on the projector. We can make s'mores over the grill." He slowed the car to make the sharp turn right.

Jason protested, pointing to the case of warm beers nestled between his feet. "Who needs a fire? We can bask in the bright, full moon. We're not abandoning tradition!"

"It's funny how much the tradition has changed." Matthew eyed the beers, Jason's extra special addition to this year's campout. The six brown bottles rattled in the thin cardboard carrier as the car continued along the road.

"This place is so quiet and empty," Rodney said with an exaggerated shudder, "kind of creepy being the only ones here. And yet, totally awesome at the same time."

As if to prove a point, Jason rolled down the window and howled as Matthew drove to their traditional campsite.

"Stop it," Matthew said. He clutched the wheel so

tight his knuckles were as white as the moon.

The campground had developed over time to add more and more sites, creating an erratic maze of sharp turns and narrow bridges along a poorly maintained dirt road. Matthew coasted more than drove, as the posted speed limit of fifteen miles per hour was impossible to achieve.

"C'mon, lighten up. I'm only having a little fun," Jason said.

Matthew parked at the designated space for their favorite camping spot, one of the original eight near the heart of the campground and about a mile from the main road. A picnic table was placed a few feet away, its brown paint weathered and chipped. Further to the right of the car was a flat space to pitch a tent. A metal pole with an empty reserved sign had *Campsite #5* etched into its rusting body, and centering the site was a newly constructed firepit made of metal and lined with stones.

Kevin and Rodney hopped out and kicked a few rocks around, looking for the best ones to throw. Jason lifted the small case of beer out of the car and handed them each a bottle. Within seconds, Rodney had started a competition with Kevin over who could throw their rock the farthest.

Jason came around to the driver's side, set the beers on the hood and peeked in through Matthew's open window.

"Are you coming? The view's awesome out here."

Matthew eyed the case of beer on the hood. Jason sighed as he removed it and placed it on the ground where it wouldn't damage the car. "Happy now?" he huffed.

Finding the courage to speak, Matthew sighed, "We shouldn't be here, Jason. We could get into a lot of trouble."

"If a ranger comes around, we'll say we meant to leave by curfew, but you lost the car keys, so we're stranded out here without cell service. Easy."

Matthew figured the case of beer would poke a few holes in his story, but he kept that to himself. "And what about the attacks? It's not safe out here after dark."

Jason shook his head. "The attacks happened miles away from here. Look. Once this weekend is over, it's over. It's gone. We'll never see it again for the rest of our lives. Let's just enjoy it while we have it."

The seventeen-year-old stared at his best friend, wishing he could convince him to leave, but knew it was no use. When Jason was set on something, that was the end of it, and he had the charisma and charm to always get his way. He wasn't wrong about the attacks, either. Grover's Pike was nowhere near where the mysterious beast had struck, and it had been about a month since the last attack.

"Alright." Matthew got out of the car, silencing the voice of reason in his mind which screamed at him to stop.

It had all started in May, when two seniors from Matthew's high school had gone to Springs Meadow after Prom, a few miles south of main street. As Susan Eckert and Peter Adams ate ice cream and stargazed on a blanket—at least that's what they were doing according to Peter—a large creature came out of the woods, tore the poor girl limb from limb, and ate her insides like she was a hot, squishy piñata. Peter fled, physically unscathed but permanently traumatized. Rangers said it was a bear attack, but Peter maintained that it was a creature he'd never seen before.

The next attack occurred in June at Camp Tree Trail, a youth camp on the west side of Cold Springs. A counselor took a group of twelve campers stargazing for astronomy patches. The official story was that a malnourished bear attacked and killed the counselor and three campers. The other nine children ran to safety while it was distracted.

The problem with crediting both attacks to a bear was that rangers and local authorities tracked wandering bears in the area, and their records showed no abnormal activity. It was probably a bear that had managed to evade tagging, but without evidence supporting the official story, rumors ran rampant.

There was even speculation of a mountain lion or pack of wolves, but by all accounts, neither of these predators had roamed the Pennsylvania landscape in the wild for around two centuries.

Whatever it was, the likelihood that the creature would strike again sent the usual bustling crowds of hikers and campers into the safety of civilization. By July all surrounding campgrounds and hiking trails within the city limits were closed after nightfall until further notice.

With the attacks in mind, Matthew circled the car, making sure all of the doors were unlocked and the windows rolled up. He considered turning the car around and backing in, but Jason was already rolling his eyes at Matthew's abundance of caution. As a final precaution, Matthew slipped the keys into his pocket, patting them for assurance he couldn't lose them. If a quick getaway did arise, he'd be ready. Matthew and Jason pulled a couple camping chairs from the trunk and set them in front of the car. They settled in and stared at the tarnished full moon in a sea of stars. Matthew tried to relax but couldn't get comfortable. Beside him, Jason cracked open a bottle of beer as if he didn't have a single care or worry.

Rodney grabbed his bag from the back seat and sat at the picnic table. Joining him, Kevin pulled out a Bluetooth speaker, unconcerned about the risks.

The growing fear of death lingered on Matthew's mind as a soft chill of the late-August night teased the brown tufts of his hair. The moon drifted across the sky, inching its way toward the mountainous horizon, its heavenly glow illuminating everything Matthew could see. He tried to appreciate the beauty rather than fixating on the terrors his surroundings could conceal.

"Man, can you believe it. Senior year," Jason said, half amazed, half irritated.

Matthew gave a halfhearted response. "The nine-month countdown to complete freedom begins on Monday."

Jason chuckled and slouched in his chair, balancing the brown bottle against his belly. "I don't see how college can be considered freedom. It's more like going from jail to the state penitentiary." He laughed heartily at his own joke and adjusted his chair, searching for even ground. The beer bottle tipped precariously in his hand as he wrestled with the chair. Matthew flinched to the side to avoid getting spilled on and grabbed the bottle, jerking it upright. Jason laughed harder. He had too many freckles to count, and his bright blue eyes appeared almost white in the moonlight. He didn't worry about consequences, so Matthew had to worry enough for the both of them.

"And besides," Jason continued, satisfied with his steadied chair, "how are we going to travel the country if you're stuck in class all day?"

Matthew rolled his eyes. He wanted out of Cold Springs as much as Jason did, but Matthew's plans involved Penn State's biology program. Meanwhile, Jason dreamed of driving a beat-up van wherever they felt like going and stopping at every kitschy roadside attraction along the way. An end was inevitable when it came to Matthew's friendship with Jason. The thought saddened him, but he also acknowledged how a part of him would feel relieved and excited to be truly on his own.

"I can't wait to graduate and actually do something with my life and not get stuck here like everyone else.

But for now, I'm just worried about you staying out of detention so we can make the most of senior year," Matthew said.

Jason chuckled, but Matthew wasn't joking. Jason got into trouble often, but he found his way around most of the fallout. Stealing the beer would probably get him grounded for a month, but he'd convince his parents to make exceptions until they forgot he was grounded. He didn't have as much success with school administrators, but detention was more like a social hour according to Jason and his fellow regulars.

Rodney got his speaker paired to his phone, and the synthesized notes of an 80s pop song drifted into Matthew's ears. It's beat found the tips of his fingers, and he drummed against his thigh while his feet twitched to the melody. But it wasn't enough to distract his troubled thoughts about the attacks and the risk of getting caught trespassing.

Jason took another swig and noticed the nervous look on Matthew's face. "Yeah, well, I can't send you out into the world until you've learned to relax and enjoy the moment." He motioned to the beautiful view of the small campsite. "Look at this place. It's awesome!"

"Fine," Matthew snapped, tired of being told to

relax. "Get the lanterns, we need a little more light."

Jason got out of his chair and went to the trunk, pulling out the battery-powered lanterns they'd brought with them. Clicking them on, he placed them in the firepit, the light piercing the darkness with sterile white beams, then returned to grab another beer.

"I'll be back. You take it easy," Jason demanded as he joined Rodney and Kevin at the picnic table.

Mathew sat alone, watching a soft mist rise along the ground as the cool night air wisped between the trees. Crickets chirped, and an occasional hoot or caw echoed from the surrounding darkness. Every noise, no matter how innocent, made Matthew's heart race a little faster. He wished he could turn off the anxiety like his friends who joked and laughed at the picnic table. He opened an offline game on his phone to distract him, but mostly his attention focused on the clock ticking off the time from the corner of his screen.

Fifteen minutes later, Jason returned to offer him a beer. "Come hang out with us, you're totally killing the vibe."

Matthew scowled at the bottle as Jason waved it high above him.

"I can't relax," Matthew said, his voice cracking as

he steadied his trembling fingers. "We shouldn't be here. This place is restricted, and for good reason. Also, I'm the designated driver, remember?"

"Calm down, Matty. You're always playing it safe."

Matthew shook his head. "I have to play it safe, for all our sakes."

"How are you still obsessing?" The intensity of Jason's voice gripped Matthew's chest like a vise. "The bear has had a whole summer to gorge itself. We're fine."

"Peter said he saw—"

"Peter was probably high or buzzed the night the bear attacked, and now he's had some kind of mental break from the trauma. I feel for the guy, but he didn't see a monster."

Matthew's voice caught in his throat. "Susie got killed because she didn't know what was out there. The others died because they thought the attack was a one-time thing. Why are we taking the risk?"

Jason clenched his jaw and glanced over Rodney and Kevin, who'd wandered into the open area and resumed chucking rocks into the darkness.

Returning to his chair, Jason let out an irritated sigh. "Look. I wanted tonight to be *fun*." He emphasized the word fun as if to command Matthew to enjoy the evening. He motioned to their two friends, now aiming their rocks at a pole identifying campsite #3. "They get it. I don't understand why it's such a big deal to you?"

Matthew straightened his back and wiped his sweaty palms on his pants. There was no point in trying harder to explain himself to Jason. "I want to go back. It's getting really late, and I've got things to do."

"You've got things to do?" Jason asked, offended. "What's more important than hanging out with your friends?"

Before Matthew could give him a reasonable explanation, a rock hit the Campsite #5 pole and ricocheted, clanging against the car's passenger side door. Matthew jumped out of his seat, then heard the chorus of laughter from Rodney and Kevin, who stood in the shadows of pine trees.

"He was actually aiming for you," Rodney said, pointing at Kevin while still holding a rock in one hand. The spry young man who thought he was always centerstage of his own comedy show, wiped tears from his eyes and tried to get a breath in between his rolling laughter.

"You two jumped like twenty feet. . . it was awesome!" Rodney exaggerated their startled reactions with his own imitation of their faces.

Jason now squatted near the front tire, inspecting the damage on the door. "You don't want to look," he said to an already frazzled Matthew.

Matthew reluctantly joined him, using his phone flashlight to find the chipped paint. "My dad is going to flip when he sees what you did, *Rodney*," he called. Of all the ways he could get into trouble tonight, Matthew hadn't considered car damage.

"I don't know, Matthew, it looks like it's an improvement!" Kevin laughed, tossing his empty beer bottle next to the lanterns in the cold fire pit. He pushed up his glasses and lumbered around in search of another rock.

Matthew resisted the urge to remind him where the bottles should go and shook his head. "Keep the rocks in that direction, please." He pointed toward the woods, away from the car. He noticed trembling in his outstretched arm and hugged it to himself.

"Ok, dad," Rodney said in a low, mocking voice.

Kevin and Rodney continued chucking rocks against the nearby trees and howling at the full moon, completely enjoying having the whole forest to themselves.

"Twenty bucks says you can't hit that tree beyond

the bend," Kevin said.

"Better be able to pay up," Rodney said, winding up like a major league pitcher.

Satisfied that no more rocks would come toward the car, Matthew squatted for a closer look. He gestured to the chipped paint and small, deep dent. "This is not okay, Jason. We need to go. Now," Matthew said. "Get everything cleaned up and everyone in the car, or I'll leave you here." It was an empty threat. Even if Matthew was imagining the danger, he'd never leave his friends unprotected, and Jason knew it.

"Hey, you guys!" Jason called. "Let's pack it up. Matthew wants to get going soon." His tone was less empathetic and more trickster, but at least he was moving the party closer to home.

"Just a second!" Rodney lobbed the small rock, hitting his expected target and celebrating with a boisterous howl.

Kevin aimed for another tree a few feet beyond and chucked the rock. When the loud thunk confirmed his hit, he too let out a loud cheer, waving his hands wildly.

Matthew's stomach churned at how much noise they were making. If there were any rangers around, they'd be looking for the source of noise. He and Jason tossed the camp chairs back into the trunk, and Matthew slammed it shut. "You guys we really need to—"

Matthew's protest immediately halted when a shrill cry came from the distant woods. The pitch didn't sound human or even animal. It was melodic, but tortured, like a flute being fed through a shredder.

"What was that?" Matthew asked, his heart knocking against his ribs so fiercely his chest ached.

Jason shrugged. "Maybe a coyote or something."

The sound came again, echoing through the forest like a faint war cry. Kevin and Rodney had frozen in place.

"That wasn't a coyote," Matthew breathed. He stepped out from behind the car and motioned for Rodney and Kevin to move. But they ignored him and peered into the forest with reckless curiosity.

Tree branches cracked and popped. Crickets chirped, and mosquitos zipped. Even the moon hummed. Every little noise pulsed adrenaline through Matthew's body like sonar.

"Maybe it's a siren. I bet Sheriff Rhoades is on his way!" Jason joked.

"If my dad finds out I'm breaking the law…" Matthew opened the driver's side door and honked the horn at

Rodney and Kevin, his desperation to flee overriding his desire to avoid loud noises. "Grab everything, and let's go!" He turned on the headlights and flicked them on and off to emphasize his point, leaving them on to illuminate the campsite.

Jason laughed as he set the last remaining two bottles of beer in the cupholders and weakly tossed the empty box back toward the picnic table. He was worried, but whether of the sheriff or a monster, Matthew didn't know.

The shriek sounded again. Kevin and Rodney grabbed the lanterns, and Jason collected the speaker and backpack still at the picnic table. Matthew's shaking hands and stiff fingers fumbled with the keys, unable to control his panic. It was the monster for sure. Matthew pushed the key into the door but stopped when something broke through the bushes.

A large bull elk leapt into camp making Rodney and Kevin yell and trip over themselves. Kevin toppled and pulled Rodney down with him.

The behemoth of fur and muscle zig zagged through the camp, almost stomping on Kevin as it searched for a way out of the clearing. Rodney pulled Kevin over to him, as they huddled on the ground, clutching each other into a tight ball and protecting their heads.

Jason dove into the passenger seat and slammed the door shut. The elk darted back and forth in an erratic pattern. In the headlights, its massive antlers created eerie shadows against the trees as enormous hooves dug into the soft dirt. Finally, the animal leapt across the camp and dove into the forest.

Next to Matthew, Jason released his breath slowly. "I think I peed a little," he confessed.

Matthew rested his forehead against the wheel and slowed his heaving chest. "I think I did too."

They exchanged glances. Their tight lips softened into smiles, and quiet chuckles dissolved the tension between them.

Rodney and Kevin's relieved laughter echoed across the campsite, helping to ease the tension as well.

"I don't think it was the sheriff." Rodney snorted as he stood and glanced at Jason and Matthew in the car. He and Kevin started gathering the lanterns they'd dropped, their movement slow and uncertain.

"I think those idiots are drunk," Jason said.

"Or they were almost killed by an elk." Matthew resisted the urge to say *I told you so*.

With the lanterns gathered, Kevin patted his side

pocket of his jeans and called out, "I dropped my phone." He and Rodney started retracing their steps, waving the lanterns over the ground as they searched.

"Kevin almost got trampled," Jason said, suddenly serious. As his adrenaline faded, reality replaced the void bringing a cold truth with it. "He could have died." Jason didn't try to hide his shaking hands. "I think it's time to leave now," he said.

Matthew's body finally relaxed when he heard Jason say *leave* with such sincerity. "Thank you," he said with a relieved smile.

Jason smirked. "Don't look so happy, the night is still yo—"

"Ahhhhhhhh!" Kevin yelled from across the camp. Rodney screamed a string of profanities.

Matthew looked over the dashboard to see a blur of teeth and claws pinning Kevin to the ground. In a heartbeat, Rodney's yelling turned to screaming. The cocktail of booze and shock delayed his desperation to run. Wide eyed, his mind only had moments to study the carnage displayed before him.

A massive creature the size of a black bear huddled over Kevin, blocking him from view and separating Rodney from the car.

The beast's long, bristled tail swept over the dirt, swirling dust in the headlights that settled against its dark, brown pelt. When it moved aside, Matthew gasped at the sight of Kevin lying still and silent, his throat violently torn, his head dangling to one side. The hairy creature chewed on the soft fleshy parts of his torso. Its snout, dripping with blood, dug deeper into Kevin's rib cage like a pig foraging for truffles. A wet gurgle of satisfaction echoed from the creature as it lapped up blood and gnawed on the organs.

Kevin was dead.

Beside Matthew, Jason dry heaved. The sound brought Matthew out of his stunned paralysis, and he turned the ignition. They needed to leave. Now. Maybe he could drive around the creature and pick up Rodney. Or should he try to ram the beast?

The engine roared to life, and the beast's head snapped to the direction of Matthew's car, its eyes glowed orange like fiery embers.

Rodney raced toward the car and dove into the back seat, sparing Matthew the decision.

Jason smashed the automatic locks. The mechanical *click* gave him a sense of security, though it wouldn't protect him any more than a sheet protected a child from the boogieman beneath their bed. To the creature, the three boys in the car probably looked like dinner in a tin can.

"Go! Go!" Rodney said as he beat his hands against Matthew's seat.

Matthew looked toward Kevin's eviscerated body to get eyes on the monster. The creature had abandoned its prey, leaving Matthew's friend resting in a pool of blood and mud. His eyes gaped open behind broken glasses, staring in the distance.

"Guys," Rodney said, his whiny voice breaking at the top of his throat. "Where did it go?"

Assuming it had retreated into the nearby shadows, Matthew peered into the darkness toward the exit, trying to gauge whether it was safe to drive in that direction. It was as if the thing had vanished into thin air.

Matthew decided to go for it. Even a tin can was deadly if someone threw it hard enough, so if the beast was waiting to ambush, Matthew could count on momentum turning the car into a ramrod. He turned the wheel and pressed hard on the gas to back out of the parking stall, his tires sending small rocks clanging against the undercarriage. As he shifted into drive, a large, clawed hand punched through the rear passenger window and grabbed Rodney by the neck, prying the boy from his seat and out into the darkness.

Amid the chaos of shouts and profanities, Matthew's survival instinct kicked into the highest gear. Rodney was probably already dead, and Matthew had to get him and Jason to safety. He hit the gas and tore into the dirt road connecting the campsites. The exit sign reflected brightly in the headlights like a lighthouse in a turbulent storm. Matthew steered straight toward it, disregarding the road's boundaries so he could get more traction from the hardpacked dirt.

Matthew kept his eyes ahead. "Is it following us?" he asked Jason.

"I don't know, I don't see anything."

Matthew retraced the way he'd taken into the campground, driving his car through sharp turns, steering around deep divots, and gingerly crossing a narrow bridge. Adrenaline thickened his blood, and he gripped the wheel like an F1 driver, his mind a slurry of fear and determination. He saw the main road in the distance. He was so fixed on getting out of there, he didn't notice the steep drop along the shoulder of the last turn.

"Oh no!" Matthew jerked the wheel to bring the car fully onto the dirt road. The car skidded out, high centering on a raised embankment.

Dust danced in the headlights as Matthew's trembling hands shifted into reverse. He floored the accelerator, but the tires didn't move. The engine roared when he tried again. An overwhelming panic took him and tears threatened to fall.

"Get out and push," Matthew commanded.

Jason gave his friend a sharp look. "Are you crazy!"

"We have to do it now before that thing catches up."

Jason raised a finger and pointed out of the windshield. Two glimmering orange orbs caught in the headlights. The charging animal bounded on all fours through the woods and took a flying leap onto the car. The boys screamed as its head crashed through the windshield, the tempered glass bending beneath its weight.

The force of impact was enough to dislodge the car from its barrier.

The creature roared and wriggled its head free. It filled the glass hole with its meaty, human-like hand and long arm, reaching inside and grabbing Jason's shirt.

"Matthew!" Jason screamed as the creature pulled him against the dashboard. He grabbed at the bottle in the closest cupholder and smashed it against the creature's arm. This split second gave Jason enough time to recline the seat fully and scramble into the back. He started throwing anything within reach at the beast's arm to distract it from Matthew in the driver's seat.

Matthew revved the engine, and the car jerked away, straining under the creature's bulk. Matthew kept the momentum steady until the car's tires hit the asphalt of the main road.

"Hang on!" Matthew accelerated to fifty miles per hour and hit the brakes hard. The monster tumbled off the hood of the car and onto the side of the road. Matthew immediately sped away. The eerie howl of the wind through the hole in the windshield filled the car.

Jason pulled a few fingers through the tear in his shirt and tried to process what had happened.

Kevin and Rodney were dead. It didn't matter that the car was trashed or that the boys had broken numerous laws and rules. Matthew's dad was his least concern now. How would he ever face Kevin and Rodney's families? He should have pushed harder against the trip. Why hadn't he stood up to Jason?

"Call 911 as soon as we're back in range," Matthew yelled over the wind. Tears had started to fall, and the gale in the car dried them instantly on his cheeks, but he didn't care. He continued speeding along the road, silently praying whatever that monster was, remained in the forest.

The Saturday morning sun lifted over the mountains, rising like fresh baked bread, its light buttering the clouds with golds and pinks. Creeping along the treetops, the rays reached into the valley, filling the nestled town of Cold Springs with warmth.

The once booming coal-mining town had suffered irreparable disaster with the collapse of two mines, the first in 1982 and the second two years later. The tragedies had killed forty miners, and the loss of work opportunities left many residents in financial ruin. People moved away, depleting the population to roughly a fourth of what it once was. Without the mines, the town leaned into the recreation industry, its economy dependent on tourists visiting the many campsites in the surrounding wilderness.

Liam Fredricks, a handsome thirty-something with

a pension for disaster, had researched the town's history, so as he drove the last few miles to Cold Springs, the tell-tale signs of abandoned homes struck him as a death knell for a community already hanging on by its fingernails.

The northern wall of an old barn bore a large American flag mural and a bright welcome sign. At the town's center, a yellow water tower loomed overhead, the town's name painted in white along the large bowl. Throughout Cold Springs, aspen and oak trees mingled with pine and fir, littering the town with shade and seclusion. Houses with deep yards lined the many streets which wound like a maze. Many roads came to dead ends at the forest's edge, planned expansion that Cold Springs never achieved.

Seeing a gas station sign in bright neon lights, Liam pulled in. He still had half a tank, but until he could check into his accommodations, he might as well mingle with some locals.

In the next stall over an old man waited at the pump as he filled his truck. Deep wrinkles lined his tanned face and a bright orange hunter's hat covered tufts of white hair. Liam popped open the access panel to the gas tank and got out to stretch his legs.

After selecting his fuel, he leaned against the car

and made eye contact with the man.

"Just passing through?" the old man asked.

"I'll be staying at the Hubby Hole for a few days. Any suggestions for what I should do while I wait for check-in time?"

"Besides camping in the most scenic place west of the Alleghany River, there isn't much else to do around here. It shouldn't be a problem to check in early, though. There are only ever about three cars in the parking lot of the Hubby Hole." He laughed and shook his head. "You must have family in town if you're sticking around so long. I doubt there's anyone you might know who lives here."

Liam cringed when the man said *family*. "I'm actually hoping to learn more about the what's going on with the attacks."

"You a reporter?"

Liam shrugged, his bright green eyes reflecting the morning sun's light. "Something like that. Care to give me your impressions of what's happening?"

"Bear attacks." A pensive look washed over the man's face as he withdrew the nozzle from his truck and screwed the gas cap back on. "Probably rabies."

Liam watched him step into his vehicle. "That's

good to know," he said, waving goodbye. "Have a good day." The pump abruptly stopped, and Liam returned it to its slot.

On the northside of town, the Hubby Hole's parking lot was indeed empty, even though it was the only motel in town. Bright teal railings accented two-floors with ten doors on each level. The Hubby Hole was a sight to see, to say the least. Liam waited to turn left into the parking lot until a flatbed truck carrying a vehicle had passed in the oncoming lane. A large tarp covering the car billowed at the sides, revealing a flash of red.

As he pulled into the parking lot, Liam noticed bear figures scattered around the property. At the lobby entrance, a black bear made of plaster held a fishing rod over a cement pond, the dumbfounded look on its face suggesting it didn't realize the fish were painted on the cement. More plaster bears stood between the doors to the guest rooms. They sported suits, ballerina tutus, binoculars, and other nonsensical clothing and accessories. Each bear had the same goofy grin with their pink tongues wagging behind the long canine teeth. The rooms' wooden doors featured carvings of bear heads, their mouths housing peepholes.

Like the old man had predicted, Liam had no trouble

checking in, though his arrival at the front desk startled the middle-aged woman dozing behind the counter. She smiled flirtatiously at the tall blond and glanced at his barren left ring finger as she handed him his key.

Liam had expected a key card, so an actual key on an actual keyring gave him some indication of what lied ahead. Though he wasn't much of a design critic, he gawked at the room the moment he stepped through the door.

Pictures of moonlit landscapes filled the wood-paneled walls of the small room. A musty smell clung to the polyester furniture, and a thin layer of dust blanketed the lamp fixtures and picture frames. Once shaggy, the purple carpet lay matted with water stains near the bathroom door. Atop a cheap panel dresser, a large-screened TV rested beside a DVD player, with a laminated sign which read *See front desk for movies*.

He reluctantly set his carry-on against a small desk in the far corner and sat on the bed. Thank heavens it was comfortable. This room would meet his basic needs, which at the moment was sleep.

He'd gotten back to his cabin near Blood Moon a little after midnight and tried unsuccessfully to sleep. He felt anxious about the trip, but it was an unexpected rush of grief that denied him rest. When he hadn't managed to doze off by the time his clock read three in the morning, he'd finally decided to pack his bag and drive the four hours to Cold Springs rather than stare at the ceiling until sunrise.

It had been two years since the horrible night he lost his wife, Leslie, and their daughter, Ruth. Some days their loss felt barely hours old, other days it felt like two long years marred with nightmares. He couldn't stop dwelling on the night they died, his mind racing through all the what-could-have-beens, and if-onlys.

Friends and loved ones couldn't understand his grief. Rather than face their constant questioning of why he hadn't moved on, he purposefully isolated himself. He'd found comfort in grief support groups, because fellow survivors dealt with the same frustrations, but eventually every session felt like a slightly different version of the same meeting, so he stopped going.

There'd been nothing out of the ordinary that night at his parents' cabin in the Maine countryside. They'd purchased it a couple of years after retiring, and every other year since, Liam, his three siblings, and all of their spouses and children gathered there for a long weekend of hiking, fishing, and four-wheeling. In the evenings, the whole family sat around the outdoor fireplace for little talent shows, pleasant conversation, and plenty of snacks. It was a chance to catch up with everyone's busy lives and take it easy from a fast-pacing world.

The two-level cabin with a wrap-around deck presented the beautiful Appalachian Mountain view of golden sunrises and crimson sunsets, but its three bedrooms filled up quickly when the whole family arrived. The grandkids had taken to having cousin slumber parties in the living room, and Liam's sister and brother-in-law were a pair of city dwellers through-and-through who called dibs on one of the spare bedrooms. His other sister took up residence in the remaining spare bedroom, keeping mostly to herself. This left Liam and his youngest brother, Danny, to enjoy camping outside with their wives and any of their kids who preferred a tent to the cousin party. Liam set up camp in a space beside a homemade swing while Danny's family settled farther across the yard.

Liam could recall details of that night with stunning clarity. He'd examined and reexamined them, searching for what he could have done differently, wishing someone could have warned him or prevented it in the first place. The what-ifs had kept him in the grip of crippling insomnia and restlessness. Now that he'd reached Cold Springs, where he hoped to make the difference he wished someone had made for him, his exhausted mind refused to rest. Instead, it did just the opposite, buzzing like the AC unit beside the bed.

He sank into the memories. He'd denied them for a few weeks now, and maybe, if he gave them some attention, they'd fade enough for him to get some sleep. He leaned back on the bed and closed his eyes, setting the vivid memories free.

He's sitting by the fire on the cabin grounds. It's late, and most of the family has drifted off to bed in tents or inside. Liam, Danny, their father, Leslie, and a few children remain. Danny strums his guitar. The air has cooled, and Liam snuggles close to Leslie, a fleece blanket wrapped around them both. They wait patiently for Ruth to grow tired enough to be put to bed. The petite five-year-old with strawberry blonde curls and bright blue eyes sits in front of Danny's eldest daughter, Lindy, who's braiding Ruth's hair. Both girls sing quietly to the soft music.

The night breeze twists the leaves in a chorus of rattles, and the crackling fire keeps his feet warm. Liam's father offers to share a story with the children about their rambunctious fathers, and everyone listens intently. They're all stories Liam has heard before, but watching Ruth hearing them for the first time and trying to understand the idea of him being a kid brings a smile to his face.

Liam relishes this moment of peace, as he's struggled to find any lately. He and Leslie lived with their daughter in Augusta, Maine, where he'd started a program for troubled teens and worked as the lead youth counselor. Before leaving for the weekend, he'd learned two more of the kids had been arrested again. Was he really the right person for this job? Why couldn't he get through to them?

Leslie looks into Liam's green eyes and playfully rubs the back of his neck. The caramel light of the fire brightens her auburn hair and paints gold highlights in her hazel eyes. He still can't believe he'd convinced her to marry him.

"You, okay?" she asks. "You went away for a minute."

Liam flashes a halfhearted smile. "Just thinking about work."

She snuggles her face into the crook of his neck. He'd filled her in on the arrests during the car ride to the cabin. "You've helped so many kids and families. But there's so much you can't control in their lives and the choices they make. You'd connected with those two kids. I'm sure they're worried about disappointing you."

"I get it," Liam whispers back. "I'm worried I'm disappointing you."

Leslie nudges him and tilts her head to kiss his cheek. "You never could."

Liam hugs her closer and gazes into the fire. She's probably right about the kids. He decides to go visit them after the weekend and offer them the same loving assurance that Leslie just gave him. At the very least, they'll know they always have a place in his program.

Danny stands. "Lindy, it's bedtime."

Both Ruth and Lindy groan, and Grandpa waves his hand. "No worries, girls. I saw Grandma hide the last ice cream bar in the freezer. How about we split it three ways before bed?"

The two girls follow Grandpa toward the cabin, and Liam admires Lindy's artwork atop his daughter's head. She's woven Ruth's hair into rows of fishtail braids that slowly unravel at the ends.

A few minutes later, Grandpa returns with Ruth, who rubs her tired eyes and yawns. The small girl reaches for her mother, who pulls her into her arms.

"Lindy's joining the cousin slumber party, but Ruth said she wanted to be with you," Grandpa says.

Liam exchanges a glance with Leslie. They'd been working on easing Ruth's separation anxiety, and her decision to forgo a sleepover suggested she still needs time. Liam gladly gives it to her. She'll be a moody teen who demands her distance soon enough, so he cherishes these moments when she needs him.

Leslie balances Ruth in her arms. "I'll get this fairy tucked away into her magical sleeping bag, and then I'm calling it a night. Are you staying up longer?"

It's almost one in the morning, and he wants to be somewhat alert for fishing the next day. "I'll help get things put away out here and catch up in a few minutes."

He and Danny send their father back into the cabin and set about putting away the last few bags of snacks, throwing out the trash, and dousing the fire.

Checking the time, Liam returns to the tent. It's a little past 1:30 AM. This version of himself two years ago has no idea that his nights of deep sleep are gone.

As he starts to drift to sleep on his cot, the soft whistle of wind makes the tent gently sway around him. In what feels like only seconds later, he wakes to the sound of screams.

In the Hubby Hole, Liam's eyes snapped open, bringing him back to reality. "Don't think about it." He spoke the words aloud and sat up in the king-size bed. He rubbed his face and stretched his stiff back. "She wouldn't want you to dwell."

Liam slipped on his shoes—he didn't trust his bare feet on the matted carpet—and retrieved his laptop from his suitcase. Leslie might not have wanted him to dwell, but he couldn't help himself, not after letting his walls down and letting in so much of the memory. He sat at the desk and opened the laptop.

The monitor portrayed a happy family portrait of him, Leslie, and Ruth. They huddled together in a beautiful clearing, wearing pastel pink and yellow. The moment captured Ruth giggling, her hands clasping a white Gerber daisy, and Leslie and Liam reacting to her. It was Liam's favorite picture.

Liam's heart ached as he took a moment to stare at the image. To say life was unfair would be an understatement, but Liam was never one to play a victim. He couldn't get them back, but he could help prevent other families from suffering like he did.

From the touchpad, Liam opened a single folder

in the upper right corner labeled COLD_SPRINGS_ KILLER. He scrolled through the documents, images, and videos he'd collected over the past six months. The collection started in February when Liam first read about the slaughter of five people in Oxford, Maine, and recognized similarities to the death of his wife and child.

Though locals of Cold Springs believed a rabid bear was on the loose, Liam believed the deaths were man-made, thus his use of words like *killer* and *murder.*

Creating this trove of information had become an obsession, an unhealthy one. But contrary to what his friends and family thought, this wasn't about revenge.

He couldn't have revenge even if he wanted it. The man who'd killed Leslie and Ruth had long since been dead. Liam had witnessed his demise. But the recent attacks convinced Liam that there was someone else out there like the killer, but the authorities lacked an awareness of the true nature of the evil. What Liam had seen when he survived the attack at his parent's cabin put him in a unique position to stop it.

A few months after the attack, Liam had sold his house. He'd taken his inheritance and life insurance money, and moved to a cabin twenty minutes outside of the quaint town of Blood Moon, Pennsylvania to hide from the world. He lived frugally, worked seasonal jobs, and occasionally consulted for the local psychiatrist. But when he'd found the report of five people dead in an apartment in Oxford, he couldn't hide any longer, at least metaphorically speaking. He hadn't exactly rejoined civilization, but he had spent every spare moment scouring the internet with the goal of finding and stopping the serial killer.

He'd found two attacks in February. The one in Oxford included a description of a large man in a puffy coat.

Two nights later, three more people were found mutilated at a bus stop in Conway, New Hampshire. Fuzzy security footage released by an undisclosed source on YouTube showed a burly man in a big, puffy coat slashing at the victims with some kind of multitool, and when Liam saw it, he knew the apartment slaughter wasn't an isolated event.

In March, in Amherst, Massachusetts, four teens were found near Puffers Pond, their bodies almost unidentifiable. The kids were out on a double date and decided to take a stroll after dark. No eyewitnesses had come forward, but the medical examiner ruled it an animal attack, perhaps a bobcat or a bear.

In April, three men were killed in a parking lot at the local bar in New Haven, Connecticut. Eyewitnesses claimed a man with knives attacked swiftly and mercilessly from the dark. The murderer vanished before anyone could stop him.

And then in May, two teens were attacked, in Cold Springs, Pennsylvania, leaving one dead. With this attack, the narrative turned firmly toward a rabid bear on the loose.

In June, the killer struck again in Cold Springs, murdering a counselor and three kids. The local sheriff chalked the deaths up to a territorial bear wandering in the woods and would not comment on whether the investigation connected this attack to the one on Prom night. There was plenty of gossip in the comments section of the article, but nobody proposed the possibility of anything other than a bear.

According to the online reports, law enforcement was still searching for the killer in Connecticut, and Liam assumed the same was true for the other murders.

With two attacks claiming five lives in the same small town, Liam had decided to poke around. He'd spent a few weeks preparing as best as he could and made a reservation at the Hubby Hole for the window he believed the killer would most likely attack again. He'd kept a close eye on the *Cold Spring Gazette* for updates in the meantime.

As he thumbed through the rest of his files his phone buzzed with a notification. An online article from the newspaper reported two more deaths occurred last night at Grover's Pike Campgrounds. A press conference would be held at ten that morning with more details.

Liam swore and closed his laptop.

Opening his notes app on his phone, Liam added two more names to the list of twenty victims. Now there are twenty-two victims. It's only been six months. So many grieving families and friends.

As he closed the app, a text from his mom came through telling him to be safe on his drive to Cold Springs. He'd informed her of his road trip but she didn't know he'd done the drive in the middle of the night instead of early morning. He immediately replied that he'd already arrived and was excited to take a dip in the motel pool later that afternoon.

He added a smiling emoji, hoping she wouldn't attempt a lengthy conversation.

She responded with a heart emoji and wished him well on his little vacation. She requested he send a postcard for her fridge and ended with *I love you.* This was the way of their conversations over the past two years. Liam kept things from her. She knew, but she also knew better than to push him. They'd fallen into a rhythm of using small talk and emojis to maintain some semblance of closeness, and the words *I love you* covered everything else.

Liam replied *I love you too* and promised a postcard was on its way. He felt strangely comforted by the knowledge that someone knew where he was and would notice if he vanished. He deleted the conversation immediately.

He wasn't sure what was going to happen during his time in Cold Springs and couldn't risk emotional distractions. He needed to be ready for anything.

The press conference would start in about an hour, and Liam wanted to be there to get a good look at the people in the crowd. His stomach growled, reminding him he hadn't eaten since his early dinner the day before, and for him to find something to eat before heading to the town hall.

He packed his laptop and grabbed his carry-on. He'd be staying at least two nights, but didn't want to leave his belongings in the room. Someone might get curious about the nosy stranger and break in, or if he had to flee, he wouldn't be able to collect his things.

He locked his room, headed to his car, and popped open the trunk. Carefully placing the carry-on to one side, he took inventory of the other objects there.

Liam wanted to be prepared for anything and stocked up on rope, zip ties, and a net. The net was probably unnecessary but he was an internet sleuth riding an office chair, and an amateur one at that. He wasn't exactly sure what he was doing on this hunt. He'd pushed his shotgun out of sight toward the back. Though he'd only ever shot at targets and cans, he figured he could aim and pull a trigger just fine if it came down to self-defense.

Liam's bigger problem was that he hadn't yet figured out what to do if he actually caught the guy. His mind wandered to the dark possibility of killing the murderer, but he relinquished the thought immediately. He was figuring this out as he went, and he had to trust himself to make the right decision in the moment.

His stomach growled once again, and he pulled the trunk door closed.

A large room in the Cold Springs town hall buzzed with the crowd of people and reporters filing into several rows of folding chairs. A wide aisle parted the rows down the middle.

Liam had planned on standing toward the back where he could study the crowd, and he nonchalantly leaned against the far wall near a few others trying to stay out of the way. He watched reporters from the neighboring towns taking their places with their press passes and digital recorders, jostling for position in the front rows reserved for the press. Different news logos and matching microphones decorated the podium at the front of the room.

"Looks like a full house," Liam said to a local woman standing nearby.

"Every time there's been a death, the mayor has

called a town meeting to discuss things with the forest rangers," the local said. "I think they do it to assure us we're not in danger, but they're doing a terrible job."

Liam chuckled as he glanced over the large space. The chairs filled up fast, and people began leaning against the walls or sitting on the floor.

"If you're press, you should put on your badge and get up there," the woman said.

Liam should have known he couldn't blend in at a small-town gathering. "I'm not a reporter." He considered lying and saying he was a blogger or just someone passing through, but he realized he'd probably need to ask questions during his time there. Misrepresenting himself would damage other's trust. "I've been studying the attacks. Consider me a fly on the wall."

A group of city officials walked to the front table, each taking a seat as cameras flashed and locals grumbled. The response took Liam by surprise. It seemed the woman wasn't the only one displeased by how the authorities were handling the situation.

Mayor Sheldon Whitesides approached the podium. Sweat greased his forehead and slid down his neck, though the air conditioning worked just fine. His eyes bulged from his thin face and he dabbed his forehead with a handkerchief.

After pocketing the handkerchief, he clutched the podium. All conversation stopped. The silence was heavy with anticipation.

The mayor cleared his throat and began. "On behalf of everyone working on this situation, we want to express our condolences to the Hancock and Hess families at this time. We all mourn with you and pray for your families."

Liam jotted the detailed names in his notes app. The woman looked over his shoulder and mentioned the first names of the victims. "Those boys in the front row were their friends," she whispered. "I believe they were there when it happened." Liam studied the front row and quickly found a redheaded teenager sitting next to a brown-haired boy about the same age. They both stared at the ground. Adults, presumably the parents, flanked them on either side.

The mayor continued his opening remarks. "I want to assure everyone that local rangers are doing everything possible in keeping us safe. I will now turn the time over to Sheriff Rhoades who will inform us of more details about last night's attack."

Sheriff Brandon Rhoades stood and approached the podium. He was a large man with broad shoulders and stood a little over six feet. Lean and athletic for a man in his early fifties, the sheriff clearly took pride in his health and appearance.

Looking over the gathered people and press, cameras chirping like freshly hatched chicks, the sheriff rested his hands upon the podium before speaking. "I've lived in Cold Springs all my life and never witnessed so many violent deaths since the mines collapsed in the eighties," he said. "In our town, folks pass on due to natural causes. We have an occasional accident, but with seven horrific deaths already, I don't mind admitting I'm particularly bitter at having to stand here again today.

"Thank you to those who continue to observe the restrictions we've put in place for your safety. I want to emphasize that they are working, and last night's tragic events could have been prevented. A group of teenagers was attacked by what has been confirmed to be a feral bear. We believe the animal to be the same one involved in the previous attacks. The victims and two other friends were out past curfew and trespassing on a closed campsite at Grover's Pike. Both of the victims suffered fatal trauma in the attack. Grover's Pike is an active investigation scene, and expert trackers are searching for the bear. Please avoid this area.

"I implore everyone to adhere to the restrictions in place. We will prosecute violators to the fullest extent possible, but from this tragedy, we must learn that ignoring the rules can result in far worse than a fine or a night in jail. I now invite Mr. Barkle, the head forest ranger, to present the updated restrictions. Mr. Barkle."

The sheriff stepped aside, but remained near the podium, allowing the man to address the people.

"Thank you, Sheriff Rhoades," Mr. Barkle's voice boomed. "I, too, extend our condolences to the families who have lost their loved ones. The bear doesn't show up in our system as we monitor the wildlife population in the Cold Springs area, which means it hasn't been tagged. We're working hard to locate it so it can be captured and euthanized. Until further notice, we are completely closing many trailheads and camping grounds for both public safety and to allow the trackers to do their work. We will maintain a current list on the city, police, and forest service websites and social media accounts. We will also post signs. I join the sheriff in asking everyone to mind these closures and avoid these areas. Lives depend on it. Thank you."

Mayor Whitesides returned to the microphone, joining the two officials. "We'll now take a few questions."

A dozen voices spoke at once. The mayor pointed to a reporter who stood and announced herself. "Patty Decker, *Cold Springs Gazette*. Does this attack provide any new information about the bear?"

Mr. Barkle answered the question. "It's undetermined what kind of bear is attacking, but from eyewitness reports, we suspect it's a rabid brown bear. The attacks have all occurred at night when it's impossible to accurately observe the details like fur color or actual size."

Reporters started up again, vying for the chance to speak, but this time the mayor pointed to the middle of the crowd at a woman with highlighted blonde hair pulled into a tight ponytail.

"Ms. Westbrook, you may give one comment," he sternly said.

Standing, she announced her name, "Cassie Westbrook, citizen." Many townsfolk grumbled and snorted. She twisted to scan the crowd surrounding her. When she faced Liam, he saw she had the bluest eyes humanly possible.

From viewing the videos of previous press conferences, Liam recognized her name and voice.

She'd shared the same conservation concerns at both meetings about the prior killings, and Liam expected her to repeat herself today. He was surprised the mayor had called on her at all, but the small-town politics had their idiosyncrasies. Perhaps briefly giving her the spotlight prevented bigger problems.

The footage available showed only the authorities standing at the podium, not the people asking questions from the floor, so this was the first time he'd seen Cassie. She was thin with toned muscles and wore slim gray pants, a graphic t-shirt, and green flipflops. Liam found her quite attractive, though what truly caught his eyes was a vague familiarity about her. He doubted he'd actually seen her before. Maybe she reminded him of someone. He couldn't quite put his finger on it. As he took a longer look, he tried to pinpoint any moment of seeing her bright blue eyes, a feature he continued returning to.

"I know there are procedures to follow, especially when lives have been taken, and safety is at stake, but is there another way to handle this bear without destroying it? It's only following its natural instincts and we're intruders on its territory. Perhaps if it's healthy, it can be relocated instead of destroyed."

The crowd gurgled with small conversations. The officials on stage joined the crowd's displeasure. Liam noted the sheriff's frown as he leaned closer to the microphones and stared directly at her. "I appreciate your compassion, but as I explained in the last press conference, the bear is showing a consistent pattern of deadly aggression and is likely diseased. It is protocol that it be put down before another human is attacked or it infects other wildlife."

"With all due respect, Sheriff, I only request we consider the nature of this bear and choose an alternative. And what will we do if the bear is never found? What happens the next time we encroach upon a wild creature's home, and it attacks in desperation? We should post warning signs to keep people from going where they shouldn't be in the first place."

Sheriff Rhoades chuckled. "Ma'am, we're already doing that, and yet we're here today mourning the loss of two young men. We've coexisted with bears with little incident for decades, and what we have with this bear is a severe anomaly. You've had your time, and we've heard your concern. Thank you."

Cassie ignored the sheriff's implied invitation to yield the floor. "Murder is not—"

Sheriff Rhoades cut her off, his cadence picking up speed, and his voice raising in pitch with impatience. "When we find it, we will take care of it humanely. I'm sorry you regard the life of a single, menacing animal over the seven victims, but I care more for the lives of this community than some feral creature. If you care so much about bears, perhaps you can turn your efforts toward the hundreds of bears killed by cars in this state every year."

"But *this* bear—"

"*This* bear broke straight through the front windshield of a car. It's unnatural! You haven't seen what this creature does to its victims, and you aren't the one who has to notify the families. You aren't burying a loved one. So despite what you may think, Ms. Westbrook, *this* bear has got to go."

The townsfolk nodded, expressing their support of the sheriff. Some people even clapped. A few reporters raised their hands to be called on.

Liam stepped forward, purposely interjecting, before the jockeying for the mayor's attention began again. "Liam Fredricks, out-of-towner." Sheriff Rhoades squinted at him but nodded for him to continue. "Have you considered the possibility you aren't searching for a bear but for a man? Perhaps a serial killer?"

Laughter mingled with grumbles from both sides of room. Liam had expected as much, but he wanted his theory out in the open.

Sheriff Rhoades sighed, clearly unimpressed with the quality of the questions, yet he answered sincerely. "According to the medical examiners who studied the injuries, all evidence points to bear attacks—brutal attacks, may I add. We must go where the evidence leads and not engage in unfounded speculation."

Liam respectfully nodded, thanked the sheriff, and stepped back.

Still standing at her chair, Cassie attempted to make another argument for preserving the bear's life.

The sheriff cut her off again, lifting his hand to separate them. "We have heard your suggestions and responded, Ms. Westbrook. Our decision will not change. Please, sit down."

"But if you would just take into consideration—"

"Enough!" Sheriff Rhoades's deep voice broke like thunder over the crowd, stunning everyone. His face turned two shades of red as he forced a pursed line across his face. "Euthanizing the bear insures everyone's protection, including yours."

The chirps began once again, accompanied by white flashes capturing the disappointed look on Cassie's face. In a whir of emotions, she stormed out of the exit at the back of the room, slamming the door behind her. The sheriff stepped back from the podium as Mayor Whitesides pointed to another reporter, continuing the flow of questions and answers about the previous victims and locations.

Sheriff Rhoades motioned to his deputy sitting in the front row. The two met to the side of the long table and had a whispered conversation. After the exchange of heated words, the deputy immediately made his way out of the room through the same exit Cassie had taken.

Liam made a split decision to follow Cassie. He'd gotten a good look at the crowd, and he could watch the rest of the press conference from the online recording. Cassie seemed to be the best chance for him to find out some out-of-the-box thinking. Maybe she'd listen to his theory and have some insight.

His white sneakers squeaked on the marble floors as he jogged through the main lobby and out to the street. The crisp midmorning air washed over him, the humidity already feeling like a wet heavy blanket. He found Cassie in the parking lot, unlocking the driver side door of an old Volkswagen Beetle the color of a lime popsicle.

"Ms. Westbrook." He waved his hands as he walked in between parked cars.

The woman shook her head and groaned. "Can I help you?" she asked as she held her key in the lock.

Liam took a moment to study her face, again feeling a baffling sense of familiarity. He guessed she was about twenty-five years old and a little over five feet tall. Light freckles dotted her cheekbones like footprints made by a nervous fairy in ballet slippers. Her smooth lips were tinted in pink gloss, and the rest of her face was bare—no eye make-up or concealers, no penciled in eyebrows, just her natural, sun kissed complexion. A breeze brushed the ends of her hair over her narrow shoulders. The blueness of her eyes captivated him the most, making his palms sweat.

"Can I help you, Mr. Fredricks?" she repeated. "That's your name, right?"

He looked away, realizing he was staring. "Yeah, Liam Fredricks. I don't mean to impose, but I'd like to talk. I don't think it's a rabid bear attacking the townspeople." Liam's cheeks flushed with heat from embarrassment. His burst of boldness at the town hall was the first time he mentioned the possibility of a man committing the murders out loud in public. He knew how unbelievable he sounded, and from the way Cassie narrowed her eyes at him, maybe she wasn't the sympathetic ear he'd expected.

Cassie's leaned closer to him. "Are you some detective?" she asked as she looked him over from head to toe.

"Nope," Liam said.

"Wildlife expert?" Cassie asked.

Liam gave a hushed no.

"Reporter?" She folded her arms across her chest. Her jaw tensed.

"I'm not with any specialized department. I'm not a detective or a reporter or anything like that, and I assure you I'm not some weirdo trying to hit on you."

The last bit came out unexpectedly, but Cassie didn't bat an eye lash at the remark. "Then what are you?"

"A concerned citizen. I've been following these killings, and I think the investigation is going in the wrong direction."

She remained tense, staring at him in silence for an uncomfortable amount of time. As if she were trying to read his mind, Cassie's eyes burned deeply into his.

"What makes you think it's not a bear?" she asked

slowly.

Liam opened his mouth to release a torrent of reasons and proof, but the words caught in his throat, keeping him silent and a little breathless. He debated if the parking lot was the ideal place to exchange thoughts on how the murderer was a man.

"Because Cold Springs isn't the only place these kinds of attacks occurred," he said all in one breath.

Like a t-shirt displaying various facial expressions, the look on Cassie's face went from confused to surprised to disbelief in a matter of seconds. "Shark attacks happen at many different beaches. That doesn't mean there's a serial killer on the loose." Her body relaxed entirely. "People think I'm out in left field because I don't want wildlife destroyed if there's another way, but you're not even in the right ballpark."

She grabbed the handle to open her door.

Liam stepped closer. "I've been tracking this guy. He's left a trail of evidence from Maine, and he's not just attacking in forested areas. For some reason, he's lingering here in Cold Springs. I believe the killer is still in town."

Releasing the door handle, Cassie rested her hands on her hips and sighed. "Let me guess. Your evidence comes from Google searches and YouTube videos. If your most reliable source is Patty Decker at the *Gazette*, then we're done here."

Liam didn't deny the possibility of some of the evidence being a little questionable, but he knew how to evaluate sources. His information was consistent, and he had proof. He pulled out his phone and swiped away the lock screen image of Leslie and Ruth hugging one another, the same bright filter and flower highlighting their beautiful smiles.

"There's a pattern I noticed about the killer when I put all of the events on my calendar. It has the moon phases on it, so I saw the murderer only kills around the full moon. That's how I know which killings are related."

He held up his phone showcasing a spreadsheet of full moons and murder dates.

Cassie shook her head, unconvinced. "You obviously have a lot of time on your hands, but whatever is killing innocent people is Cold Springs isn't a man and I'll prove it to you. Then you can head on back home to your lovely family and leave this poor, miserable town behind you."

Liam almost corrected her about no longer having a family, but stopped himself. He'd held his phone screen in plain sight, she'd made a reasonable assumption, and their conversation was already awkward without him raising a sensitive topic.

"Get in." Cassie jerked her head toward the passenger side.

"Are you sure inviting a stranger into your car is a safe thing to do?"

Cassie chuckled. "I'm not too worried."

Liam went around to the passenger side and got in once she'd unlocked the door. "And where are we going exactly?" he asked as he clicked on his seatbelt.

Cassie turned the ignition, the hum of the car was smooth and eager to move. "Where it all started. I'm taking you to Springs Meadow."

FOUR

assie parked her car against a wooden post which held a sign designated for patrons of Whittle's Curios and Curiosity store. Five miles away from main street, the small building was wedged between the forest and a makeshift parking lot for recreationists that was more mud than asphalt. Boulders bordered the parking lot, assuring cars wouldn't infringe on the growing fauna or drive past the natural barrier of shrubs and ferns.

The Curios was a quaint, single-level building with neon pink siding and purple shutters. Brightly colored letters were painted in the large front window, encouraging folks to satisfy their curiosity and enter. Small pinwheels stood motionless in the breathless air among fabric flowers that were bunched with ribbons and stabbed into the dry dirt beside the entrance.

Cassie exited the car and watched Maddie, a

coworker of hers, swiftly stomp out a cigarette. The teen had been taking a smoke break behind the Curios in spite of the fact that she was too young to legally smoke. Maddie kept her foot over the cigarette and tried to play it cool, brushing a strand of turquoise hair from her face.

"Aren't you scheduled for this afternoon?" Maddie asked.

Cassie pretended not to notice the cigarette, despite the smell lingering in the air. "Jeremy is working for me. I'm working his Tuesday shift."

Maddie eyed Liam as he pulled himself out of the small car and joined Cassie, taking her time to admire every inch of him. Cassie couldn't blame her. For such an odd and annoying man, Liam was strikingly handsome with thick blond hair and bright green eyes. If the sinewy forearms peeking from beneath his t-shirt were any indication, he kept himself in good shape, as well.

Liam stepped behind Cassie as if to guard himself against the unwanted attention from a girl easily half his age.

"Who's your date?" she asked.

Cassie motioned to a trailhead a couple feet beyond the parking lot. "More like a tour. Liam and I are heading to Springs Meadow."

The teen laughed as if Cassie had said the funniest joke, but her face was more contemptuous than delighted. "When you see Kyle, tell him I say hi." She ducked into the building before Cassie could ask why.

"Who's Kyle?" Liam asked.

Cassie's eyes narrowed. "Somebody I work with. He's the boss's son and does nothing but complain about how boring Cold Springs is in the summertime. I don't know what Maddie meant about telling him hi, though." She led Liam to the trailhead. "We have about a half a mile hike to Springs Meadow. It's easy. Are you ready to be proven wrong?" she asked with a hard stare.

He motioned for her to lead the way. "After you."

They passed a trail marker sign and followed a narrow dirt path leading through a thicket of trees and bushes.

After a few hundred feet, the trail widened, and Cassie slowed to walk beside Liam.

"Do you come here often?" Liam asked, trying to fill the silence. Then he blushed. "That sounded like a line. I didn't mean it like that. I'm sorry."

Cassie had noticed the picture of a woman and child on Liam's phone. She assumed they were his family, but in the car, she noticed he didn't wear a wedding band.

Usually she knew when guys were hitting on her, but Liam made no sense. Not that it mattered. She wanted him out of Cold Springs as soon as possible.

"It's fine. I like to come out here after work sometimes and relax, meditate, or star gaze. It's really peaceful and quiet, especially at night, but evening strolls are off-limits for now."

They walked in awkward silence. Tall aspens shaded the trail as sunrays lit up spaces between the fluttering leaves. Laughter from a small group echoed in the distance.

Liam scratched the back of his neck. "I made things weird, and I feel like I should explain. My wife died two years ago, along with my daughter." He spoke matter-of-factly, his words rehearsed. "I'm not dating, but women have gotten the wrong impression before, and then feelings get hurt. I worry my words might be misinterpreted as flirtatious."

Cassie felt a weight lift from her chest unexpectedly. "I think I know how you feel," she said, softening her tone. "I lost my fiancé a while back. I thought I'd never be the same after he died. We could talk about things if you'd like. I'm a pretty good listener when I'm not yelling at the sheriff."

Liam's mouth turned up into a half-smile at her attempt to lighten the mood, then he took a deep breath. "It was two years ago. I'm at peace with my loss now, but it was a long road. I'm sure Leslie, my wife, would think it awfully strange to be doing what I'm doing right now. I figured occupying my time is better than dwelling over things I don't have control over in the first place. I never thought I'd be where I'm at in my life now. We'd planned on having four kids. Ruth was an incredible daughter." He smiled. "She really set the bar high in cuteness. I was so excited to see what her siblings would be like." He paused and shook his head as if shaking himself free of her memory. "What about you? We can chat about your fiancé if you'd like."

It was a sweet gesture. Suffering a life-altering loss had a way of uniting people. Cassie's family tried to understand how it changed her, but it was something only experience could teach.

"Life's still a little difficult," she said as her voice caught in her throat. "I remember the simple things like places we went together, things we did. I cherish the dumb things that other people wouldn't understand because they were our dumb things."

"What was his name?" Liam asked, his eyes greener

than the tree's leaves.

He really did understand. Something fluttered in her chest, like a tiny star shooting across the sky and then fading with no proof of existence. Cassie's cheeks warmed and her stomach did a cartwheel. It had been such a long time since she'd said his name out loud. "Kurtis."

The trail opened to a low patch of grass before expanding into the meadow.

Springs Meadow boasted fountains of green grass, rolling mounds, and patches of wildflowers. Surrounded by a thick forest, the wide-open space could easily house a couple hundred people for special gatherings. "Here we are." Cassie widened her arms to present the meadow. "The best star gazing meadow in all of Pennsylvania and the Cold Springs version of Lover's Lane."

Cassie wasn't surprised to see other people there, but she hadn't expected so many. A cluster of about twenty people gathered near where Susan Eckert had been killed. The crowd surrounded Kyle Whittle, their phones held up high to record the thin man as he spoke. Now Maddie's comment made sense. What was Kyle up to?

Immediately Cassie's face molded to a hard scowl,

and she marched toward the group. Liam took his time following as he searched the area. If he was looking for clues, they were long gone.

As Cassie neared the crowd, she could hear Kyle's melodramatic description of the first bear attack.

"Parts of Susan Eckert were found all throughout the meadow." He rested a soft hand on his chest where his heart should have been. "She came from a good family, got good grades, and wanted to be an engineer when she grew up, but, sadly"—he paused dramatically—"the evil bear of Cold Springs had other plans."

"And Peter?" someone from the group asked, "what happened to him?"

Kyle's eyes lit up. "He barely survived. As the bear of pure evil tore Susan limb from limb, consuming her innards for a midnight snack, Peter crab crawled away from the carnage until he was able to get into his Jeep and drive away. His body was whole, but his heart was torn, having to leave behind his sweetheart, knowing he'd never see her again."

Gasps bubbled from the small crowd.

Liam came around from behind Kyle. "Would you mind going over the events again?"

"If you want to join the tour, it's fifteen bucks," Kyle

said.

Cassie rolled her eyes. Kyle was always looking to make a quick buck, just not by working his shifts at the Curios. But what did he mean by *tour*?

"I'll give you the highlights for five." Kyle waved his fingers with his palm open.

Liam pulled out his wallet without giving it a second thought and handed over a ten-dollar bill.

Kyle opened the stack of bills in his palm to make change, but Liam waved him off. Then the little weasel pointed at Liam as if recognizing him. "Your voice sounds familiar. Are you the guy from the press conference? The one who thinks it was a man who did this?"

"I want to know what wasn't in the news reports and any locations you can point out."

Kyle tucked the cash into his pocket and addressed the crowd. "Now that you know the whole story, it's a good time to take some photos or livestream to all your followers about this place. Don't forget to tag me and follow me @Kylethesmile. Let's meet back here in ten minutes."

Most of the group dispersed, but a handful remained to listen in. Kyle motioned to the ground around them. "Peter parked his Jeep right about where we're standing and took a blanket to the flat spot over there." He pointed about ten yards away in the direction of the center of the meadow. "They'd gotten ice cream from the creamery to enjoy under the stars, but from Peter's reports, they didn't finish their dessert, if you know what I mean." He raised his eyebrows, but Liam didn't respond to the juvenile joke.

Kyle let out a disappointed sigh. "A large animal came from the woods over there." He turned behind them and indicated a nearby tree line. "Peter claimed it looked like a gorilla but taller and leaner. Broad in the shoulders and chest. He was in shock, so it was most likely a malnourished or sickly bear."

"Is that what you think?" Liam asked Kyle. "It was a full moon that night, but the sky was cloudy. It would have been difficult to see what really attacked."

Kyle acknowledged Liam's question with a look of disbelief. "I think Peter's description of a gorilla is closer to a bear than a man. Susan was literally torn apart. Is any human strong enough to do that?"

Everyone's eyes glued to Liam for his response. "An incredibly strong man armed with a weapon and enraged with adrenaline could have brutalized Susan Eckert to that degree."

Cassie harumphed at the suggestion. "So a professional wrestler is what, injecting himself with adrenaline?" Her eyes went big as she shook her head at the absurdity of Liam's theory. "He must also be wearing a costume to trick Peter, a bunch of kids, and two teenagers into reporting the same description of a large animal." Her words prompted laughs from those around her.

A man in the tour group called out, "Hey, would you mind moving out of frame?" He held his phone sideways, positioned to take a photo of where the Jeep had parked. Cassie stepped beyond the lens, her feet a few inches from the deep divots made when Peter peeled out of the meadow and onto a utility road which gave access to the area.

Kyle and Liam moved several feet away, and the other tourists dispersed to look around.

"Are you still convinced that an animal is more likely than a person, yet?" she asked.

"Not in the slightest," he said with a confident tone. "Bears are pretty frightened of people, and I don't think an animal would hunt where people routinely populate, like this meadow or a campsite. A malnourished, sick, or injured animal might behave strangely out of desperation, but the attacks are separated by months and miles. To do that, an animal would have to be healthy."

Kyle folded his arms and shrugged. "Peter described an animal, not a man, plain and simple. I just don't see how anyone could confuse a human being and a bear, even in shock. But you believe what you want to. Wild conspiracies and theories are good for my business."

Cassie gave Kyle a stinging glare. "Business?"

A big smile took up half of Kyle's already goofy face as he lifted his phone and showcased a website. "I'm calling it the Cold Springs Death Tour. On the weekends, me and Richard Harding have been informing groups of people of what happened here and at Camp Tree Trail. Richard's brother will be taking on groups at Grover's Pike Campgrounds once everything settles there."

The website was mediocre, but it made Cassie's eyes narrow. With just a glance, she saw clipart of claw slashes and a snarling bear among words like *bloody* and *tragedy.* This was what created the wad of cash in Kyle's pocket. "You're capitalizing on other people's pain?"

"I'm bringing in tourists to eat at our restaurants and shop at our stores. You can thank me later for keeping your place of employment open. It's not like the trails and campsites are bringing in tourist revenue."

Cassie's disapproving look didn't faze Kyle. He excused himself to go mingle with the people.

Liam stood still, with a perplexed look on his face. He wasn't sure what to say or do.

Cassie decided to let it go, at least for the moment. As far as she knew, Kyle wasn't breaking any laws, so there wasn't anything she could do about these awful tours until she looked into the licensing requirements. She could, however, get Liam Fredricks out of Cold Springs.

"Come with me. Kyle really didn't give you your money's worth."

She escorted Liam to a large tree about twenty yards from the crime scene and pointed out five large claw marks slashed into the trunk. "Bear."

Liam ran his fingertips along the grooves. The slashes were ten inches in length and about two inches deep. As far as Cassie knew, this piece of evidence hadn't made any papers, though all the locals knew about it.

"A sharp weapon like a knife would have a narrower slash, and probably would have caught on the bark," Cassie said. "This is animal, not mechanical."

Liam's attention remained on the claw marks. He held up his hand and angled it slightly, matching each finger to a groove. Putting his back to the forest, he looked at the surrounding trees in the direction of the meadow.

"The jeep wouldn't have been in sight, and it was cloudy." Liam spoke aloud to himself. "The killer would've had to hear the kids."

He looked at the marks again. He was so deep in thought it was as if Cassie weren't there.

Seeing the claw marks on the tree felt like a sledgehammer to Liam's gut. He was no longer looking at articles or photographs. He couldn't distance himself from the traumatic reality. A girl had been brutally murdered here. Her boyfriend had watched it all. Peter's life had changed forever in an instant, and he'd been no more prepared for it than Liam.

Liam had barely survived the attack that killed his wife and daughter. EMTs took him to the hospital, where he remained unconscious for a week, blissfully unaware of his loss or how much time had passed. It could have been a second or a century.

"Oh! Liam! It's a miracle!" Liam's mother's voice is

the first thing he hears.

Liam drifts in and out of consciousness, trying to stay awake but giving in to the gentle lull of sleep more often than not. He hears snippets of voices that reassure him his family was nearby, but the two he most strains to hear, remain silent. Something is wrong, but what? Why can't he remember?

"Leslie." Liam's lips finally part after days remaining closed. He lifts his hand, finding it attached to an IV drip and is overcome with confusion. His surroundings slowly come into focus. Sterile white lights give everything a dull green hue. He's in a hospital bed. Why?

"Where's Leslie?"

Liam doesn't understand that morphine has numbed his mind. He can barely hold a thought, so he repeats Leslie's name as to cling to his focus. He frantically searches the faces of surrounding family members for any hint of Leslie's auburn hair or beautiful hazel eyes. His throat is as dry as sand and his head rattles every time his eyes dart from one face to the another.

His mother gently takes his hand and holds it. "Liam, you need to rest. You've been through so much already."

Liam looks at Mary Fredricks as if he were a young child again. "Mom? Where's Leslie? Where's Ruth?"

Mary's eyes fill with tears. Liam's father stands beside her, rubbing her arms as he stares at Liam with somber eyes.

"You three were attacked," she said. "They didn't make it, William. I'm sorry."

Liam slowly puts her words together. They were attacked. Leslie and Ruth didn't make it. She's sorry. Vague connections form, but nothing makes sense.

He tries to sit up and command his mind to work, but a wave of nausea washes over him, forcing him to rest on his pillow. Liam's head swims in a sea of words and memories, everything muffled like he's underwater. Screams. Blood. Moonlight pouring through the shredded polyester. Tent poles snapping.

Liam can't breathe. He searches for breath, but his chest won't move. Loud beeps and buzzes shout urgently around him.

"Liam!" His mother cries, but there's something not quite right. She sounds like . . .

"Liam!" Cassie spoke loudly, snapping him from the memory.

Liam blinked and removed his hand from the tree.

Cassie took her hand from his arm. When had she put it there? "Are you ok?"

Liam forced a smile as he wiped his hands on his pants. "Yep, I'm good."

"You went somewhere." She stepped back to give him some space, but the concerned look remained.

"I think I got a little too caught up imagining what happened here," he lied. He motioned to the claw marks. "This doesn't prove too much. The killer has a multitool weapon. I believe it's a mechanical claw made of multiple knives fastened to a handle. He holds the handle in the palm of his hand, interweaving his fingers between the blades. This gives him a similar dexterity to a bear."

He demonstrated by making a fist and raking his hand against the tree.

Cassie shook her head. "You are one stubborn man. I can't believe the evidence is standing right before you and you still believe a man did this."

Liam placed his hands at his waist. "I think this evidence is a bit too convenient. Maybe the killer tripped as he rushed to attack, or maybe he slashed the tree purposely to create misleading evidence. And nothing proves this slash mark occurred at the same time as the attack. So it might have really been a bear but on a different day. This is circumstantial, at best."

Cassie checked the time on her phone and sighed.

"Well, if I can't convince you that we're dealing with a crazy bear, can I at least try to convince you how amazing the food is here in Cold Springs? I don't agree with Kyle's tours, but he's not wrong about needing to spread some patronage around our local businesses."

Chuckling at the strange transition from death to dining, Liam put a hand on his stomach. He'd settled for a plastic-wrapped pastry and a cool orange juice from the gas station for breakfast. "That sounds good to me."

"And to be clear," Cassie said, "this is not a line. I'm just starving." She flashed a weak smile and Liam squinched his face into a playful cringe.

"I deserved that," he said.

They made their way back to the car, passing Kyle and his group as he took questions.

Cassie gave a rumbling sigh that made Liam smile.

"I think it's in bad taste, too," he said. "Should we turn lunch into a strategy session for bringing about the demise of the Cold Springs Death Tours?"

"I've got it covered," Cassie said as her eyes beamed in the sunlight. "Kyle probably needs some permit or official license to host tours, and if that doesn't work, his dad's a really good guy who loves this community. He won't approve of Kyle taking advantage of grieving families. You know how small towns are. They depend on each other for survival, so even when they're dysfunctional, they're still a family. They protect their own."

FIVE

It was as if Liam had stepped through time as he followed Cassie through the door of Stine's Diner, the only sit-in restaurant in Cold Springs. Classic 80s music played from ceiling speakers and stylish pictures of pop singers and rock stars hung on the walls. Black valances topped the large windows at the front of the building, accentuating the black and white tiled floor. Pink and green vinyl covered seats and benches, assaulted his eyes, matching lamps shades hung over side tables. The neon theme extended to the servers' uniform of bright green or pink t-shirts and black pants. Some even styled their hair according to the decade: puffy bangs with crimped layers, or slicked back hair parted in the middle.

It was busier than Liam had expected, maybe half full. People sat in booths or at tables, their conversations blending in a symphony of voices.

"Well this is a charming place," Liam said as he looked around. He tried to not let his face show how amused he was by the absurdity of it all. He'd expected a lot of things from a mom-and-pop diner in the middle of nowhere, but nostalgic 80s diner had never crossed his mind.

"Don't be too put off by the décor," Cassie said. "The owner has a thing for the 80s and renovated just last year. If you notice the bear statues around the Hubby Hole, they came from the old theme."

Liam nodded and laughed softly through his nose. "I had wondered about those bears."

"Go ahead and make fun—we all do. But I almost feel bad bringing you here because you're going to crave the hamburgers for the rest of your life."

A young woman with a blossom of bangs atop her head, welcomed the two and checked off a table before escorting them to a booth. Her nametag read *Cindy,* and she recited the daily special as she handed them menus.

Liam took his time glancing over the list of options. "I hear the hamburgers are the best."

Cassie took his menu and handed both back to the server. "We'll both take a number five, with steak fries and veggies," she said confidently.

"And to drink?"

"Water for me," Liam said, feeling oddly entertained by Cassie's casual demeanor. That morning she was tense and on edge, as if the whole world was against her, but now she acted comfortable and laid-back.

"I'll have a lemon-lime soda," she said.

Cindy turned and vanished into the fray of people.

Liam scanned the restaurant, taking in every amazing detail. He noticed a group of people in a booth across the room staring at him and Cassie and whispering to each other afterward. They'd probably been at the press conference. Liam did his best to ignore them and focused on Cassie's blue eyes instead.

Cassie glared at the whisperers and scooted further into the booth. "Sorry about them. It's my fault. When you go against the norm, you get a lot of attention around here."

Cindy returned with their drinks, and Liam poked his straw into the ice water. He'd wanted to broach the topic of her remarks at the press conference, and she'd given him the opportunity.

Stirring the ice in his cup, Liam said, "It is a little strange how you care more about the bear than those who have died. Normally people tend to stick up for their own species when it comes down to them or vicious animals."

Cassie responded with a half-smile and sipped her soda. "It's exactly that kind of mentality I don't like. It's not the bear's fault for wanting a little space. It's driven by instinct to protect itself or eat. I just wish we humans weren't so selfish. The more we encroach on their territory, the more this kind of thing will happen."

"Were those boys encroaching on bear territory last night?"

"Bear sightings happen out there, so yes, they were encroaching," Cassie said. "That whole campground is. And this season we need to be taking extra precautions and giving this bear more space." She paused, her eyes downcast as she picked up a cardboard coaster and tapped it on the table, deep in thought.

"That sounds like I'm blaming the boys," Cassie continued. "They were kids doing dumb-kid things. I did plenty of dumb things when I was in high school. If anyone is to blame, it's the officials. They should be doing more to enforce the curfew and restrictions."

"Kids doing dumb-kid things." Liam repeated the words softly. He rested against the neon green cushioned booth and sighed. "I'm a youth counselor—well, was a youth counselor. I don't think it's possible to stop the kids from doing dumb things, but I do believe we can help them understand there's more . . ." He paused as thoughts of the youth he once tried to desperately help flashed through his mind. "I wished the world was a much safer place for the kids to exist in."

"I'm making the same argument for the bears," Cassie said.

Liam glanced at the water filling the spaces between the ice cubes in his glass. He didn't disagree with her, but if this were really a rabid animal, he'd side with the authorities, but the evidence was clear and he knew it for a fact.

"So you were a youth counselor?" Cassie asked.

Liam was grateful for her changing the subject, but he hesitated to share more. Memories of his time with troubled youth scratched at his brain, and it hurt when they surfaced. There were so many kids so desperate to survive that they saw stealing or doing drugs as their only option. Others used bad behavior to force their parents to pay attention to them. To adults on the outside looking in, it looked like "dumb-kid things," but it was really a response to an unsafe, and unpredictable environment. They needed the basic necessities as well as love, and they'd grasp at anything resembling it.

"Well," Liam said through a long-drawn breath, "at one point in my life, I thought consistency was key in helping people. You know, showing up for them, being there when they needed to talk, advising them on what to do next, but there came a point when I accepted that it wasn't my responsibility to change them. The thing is, a quick payday from a drug deal was often more appealing than going to school so they could have a better job later—especially when they were desperate. They couldn't afford to be patient." He paused to chew his lip. "I wish I could have done better in helping them. The world isn't going to change. There will always be something more pressing, more threatening, but if I could have helped one kid see how there is more to life than quick fixes and that they could achieve a better life through hard work and diligence—maybe even a little humility and trust—then at least *their* world would be changed for the better."

His cheeks flushed with embarrassment. He hadn't opened up with someone like that since Leslie, and he felt a little guilty, as if he'd betrayed her somehow. Cassie was easy to talk to and maybe knowing that he'd never see her again had invited his honesty. Or maybe it was the synth vibes of a simpler time playing through the speakers that had encouraged him to share his thoughts with a stranger.

Cassie cleared her throat. "Is that why you're tracking a killer? Are you trying to change the world, by helping one miscreant at a time? Are you going to bring justice to Cold Springs and all the other cities who've been touched by death, by helping a killer see the better options to not killing others? You don't have a cape and cowl hidden somewhere, do you?"

Her dramatic comments made Liam squirm in his seat. He never saw himself as a vigilante. He was more of a pacifist who hated confrontation. But after the trauma of losing his loved ones and nearly dying himself, Liam knew sometimes peace and love couldn't solve the world's problems.

He was about to answer her, tell her why he decided to travel to Cold Springs, but he was interrupted by a young man approaching their booth.

"May I join you?" the handsome nineteen-year-old asked.

He stood in the aisle with his hands in his pockets. Like a California surfer, his highlighted, brown hair fell past his ears accompanying a deep tanned face and arms. His earthen brown eyes moved between the two adults as he waited nervously for a response.

"Of course," Cassie said, wide-eyed with surprise. She motioned to the space beside her. "Peter, this is Liam. Liam, Peter."

"Peter? As in *the* Peter Adams?" Liam asked, watching the young man scoot next to Cassie.

"The one and only," Peter said with a weak smile. "And you're Liam Fredricks. You've become just as popular as Cassie and me from your little interruption at the press conference. They're rebroadcasting snippets of the conversation on the afternoon news. I'm sure by tonight everyone will know who Liam Fredricks is and laugh at his random suggestion that Cold Springs is being tormented by a serial killer."

The somber look on the boy's face tugged at Liam's heartstrings. He could understand some of the boy's pain but could only imagine what it must feel like to have that pain torn open again and again by so many press conferences and relentless waves of media attention. He wondered if Peter knew about Kyle's tours.

Cindy returned with plates of food and was surprised to see the additional guest. She offered him a menu.

"No thanks." He tapped his fingers nervously on the table. "I won't be here long. But a water would be nice."

Cassie insisted he order something to eat. "It's my treat."

Giving into her persistence, Peter ordered the special of the day.

Cindy left to enter the order as Cassie stared at Peter sitting beside her.

"How are things going for you?" Cassie asked, her voice as soft as a lullaby. "I haven't seen you around much. The old ladies are missing you at church."

"I'm delaying college until Spring semester." Peter rested his hands in his lap. "Susie and I were supposed to go to Penn State together, but obviously plans have changed. My mom's not happy, but if I went, I'd just flunk out, and she'd be upset about that too."

"Still working at the mechanic?"

Peter nodded. "Just doing my best to live a normal life."

Cassie gave him a sympathetic look. "I'm glad you're keeping busy."

Liam studied his burger, feeling like an intruder in this personal moment. The bun looked homemade with a shiny, golden brown top sprinkled with sesame seeds. It was stacked high with a deep red tomato, lettuce, onions, a thick slab of cheddar, and three layers of crispy bacon.

Some kind of brown sauce spilled out of the sides, and the beef patty was easily two inches thick. It glistened with juice, and Liam knew it was cooked to perfection.

"Don't let that get cold," Peter said as Cassie's burger sat on a lettuce leaf in a sea of fries.

She brought the burger to her lips and indulged herself in a bite. Liam too, devoured the juicy piece of heaven. When the server returned with Peter's water and asked how everything was, Liam could only nod enthusiastically.

"I'm confident the rangers will catch the bear that attacked Susie," Cassie said to Peter once Cindy was once again out of earshot.

Peter shook his head. "I saw you two come in here, and I thought I should talk to Liam. I appreciated what you said at the press conference." He paused to get comfortable in his seat.

Liam finished his bite and shrugged. "I'm not sure how helpful I was."

Peter nodded. "They aren't going to find a bear. It's never been a bear."

Lifting a salted fry, Liam poked the air with it. "Exactly. It's what I've been trying to tell her. It's a serial killer. He first killed in Maine, back in February, and made his way here to Cold Springs. But for some reason, he's lingering here."

"I didn't see a man." Peter folded his arms on the table. He bit his bottom lip as if to hold back something he would possibly regret saying. "When I try to explain it, people write it off like I didn't see what I saw because I was in shock. They think I'm crazy."

"I'd say you're in pretty good company, then," Liam said. Cassie cracked a smile.

Liam continued, "I'm interested in what you saw."

Peter's knee bounced, and he took a nervous sip of his water. "It wasn't a man or a bear. It was tall and lean like a man with broad human shoulders and long human arms. Its hands had fingers with long claws instead of nails. It had the head of a wolf, long snout, pointed ears."

Peter paused and looked at Liam and Cassie, gauging their responses. Liam nodded encouragement for him to continue.

"It's the eyes I can't forget. They were orange. And not like those orange contacts people wear around Halloween, and not like the orange flash that comes when an animal's eyes reflect the light. They were glowing, almost iridescent in the shadows. I don't know how else to describe it. Anyway, it moved like a man when it stood on the balls of its feet, but it moved like an animal on all fours when it charged at us that night."

Liam looked at Cassie, who was clearly holding her tongue and waiting for him to respond.

"Peter, what you're describing—" Liam couldn't finish the sentence.

But Peter sighed. "You're both wrong about what this thing is. It's not a man and it's not a bear. The Cold Springs killer is a werewolf."

SIX

Cassie had heard of Peter's report about a supernatural monster from the local whispers and gossip, but she'd assumed it was only gossip embellished over multiple retellings or juicy tidbits taken out of context and given new interpretations. It took her by surprise to hear the nervous boy with downcast eyes identify the attacker as a werewolf.

"Look I know how crazy it sounds," Peter continued, "but it makes sense, doesn't it? Everyone thinks it's a bear because that's the most likely culprit." He pointed to Liam. "You're convinced it's a man. Though I don't know how a man would be capable of tearing a person limb from limb or punching through a car windshield. But what if what I saw was the blend of the two?"

Liam finished another fry and wiped his fingers on his napkin. "I have video footage, images, and eyewitness accounts that the killer is no less human than any of us. I believe you saw what you saw, but I suspect what you saw is a killer who is throwing people off his trail. The evidence says animal so everyone ends up debating every animal possibility and looks past the man responsible. It makes sense why you would come to such a conclusion. This guy attacks around the full moon."

Peter's eyebrows knitted together as he considered Liam's theory. Even Cassie had to admit how it made some sense, but Liam was way off base. She wondered if Liam had considered the logistics of such an elaborate ruse. The serial killer would have to be an acrobat with a mechanical engineering degree.

But even though the killer wasn't a person, if Liam could convince people it was a serial killer, that could possibly end the hunt for the bear. The authorities would have to continue keeping the trails and campsites empty to prevent the serial killer from having easy access to victims. She was beginning to like the idea.

Peter sighed. "People see what they want to see. Whatever you may be tracking, isn't a man. You're tracking a werewolf."

Liam shrugged. "Fine. But the killer has gotten comfortable in Cold Springs," Liam continued. "There are seven victims resulting from three attacks."

"Ten, actually," Peter corrected. "Three campers were found torn to shreds in July in Potter's Fork. It's about ten miles north of Cold Springs. It matches the description of all the other killings. Their families weren't expecting them home until about a month ago, so they've only recently reported it."

Cassie sat straight in surprise. "So you've been tracking it too?" She set her half-eaten burger back on its bed of lettuce. "Great."

Peter's food arrived. "It's a werewolf, not a bear. There's a pattern. Don't serial killers have patterns and fit profiles?"

Cassie adjusted in her seat and motioned to Liam. "You've got a background in psychology."

Placing his elbows on the table, Liam thought for a moment. This gave Cassie some time to take a few more bites and wonder if Peter was on to something.

Liam leaned against the table, his demeanor more animated now. He held up his hand, spreading four fingers. "Serial killers could be profiled within four categories. Some believe a higher power is telling them what to do. Then you have the type who kill for pleasure or thrill. The third targets specific kinds of people out of prejudice, and the final type kills because they want control."

Lowering his hand, Liam froze as if contemplating something he'd never considered.

"The killer isn't doing this out of prejudice. The victims don't share a common trait. We could consider control is the motivation but the pattern wouldn't fit. They're moving too fast between state borders, not to mention all the footage and eyewitnesses."

Peter had leaned in as Liam spoke, absorbing the information. Cassie's eyebrows slowly raised with doubtful interest. Was Peter actually buying this? She didn't really care what Peter or Liam thought, so long as the poor animal wasn't unnecessarily destroyed.

"So perhaps the killer is following orders from some higher power, God maybe?" Peter said. "Do werewolves believe in God?"

"Let's focus on what's more important," Liam said with a playful smile.

Liam gently bumped his fist on the table. He appeared a little uncomfortable discussing the motives behind a killer with Peter. Cassie didn't like where this was going.

"I hate to say it," Liam said, "but the brutality of

the killings makes me lean toward the type of killer who takes pleasure in what they're doing."

Peter pressed his back against the cushion and folded his arms.

"Are you okay, Peter?" Cassie asked. "Maybe this is a bit much for you take in."

She gave a compassionate look, her chest feeling a little tight as she imagined what the boy could be thinking. She glanced at Liam, hoping to communicate the reminder of what Peter witnessed only months ago.

"I'm fine," Peter said. "I guess it wouldn't matter the motivation. Susie's dead, and the monster's still out there."

"You're right," Liam said. "Let's focus on finding this guy, shall we?"

Lifting his phone, Liam showcased a screenshot of a Google map. Specific locations highlighted where each attack took place. He faced the screen to Peter and Cassie, pulling in toward the area of Cold Springs.

Cassie reached for her drink to help swallow a lump in her throat. Liam must have had way too much time on his hands. The detail of the yellow highlighted areas made her question the man's sanity.

Liam moved his finger along the screen. "The

locations trailing to Cold Springs are messy. He attacks in public places, but as soon as he gets to Cold Springs, the crime scenes are more remote, and he ditches the puffy coat for a different disguise. He doesn't have to move on because everyone's looking for a bear. He can learn this area and keep an eye on the investigation."

Cassie rolled her eyes. "Cold Springs is a small place. There's only one main road with two stop lights. Don't you think people would have noticed a newcomer showing up right as these attacks happened?"

Peter held up a hand to silence Cassie. "Not unless he's decided to live here. Sure he could have started out traveling to murder, but like you said, Cold Springs is small. It's secluded. We have miles upon miles of forest surrounding us."

Peter reached for Liam's phone, setting it on the table, and slid his plate of food aside. "Liam, our theories aren't so different. You say it's a man, I say it's a werewolf, but we're both looking for a person."

He zoomed in the image until Cold Springs was centered. "The werewolf first attacked at Springs Meadow. Then Camp Tree Trail." He pointed back to Springs Meadow and then to Grover's Pike. "Campsite #5 is the third area. Springs Meadow is the closest to town so I think that's where he starts. All the sites are easily accessible by trails, and see how all of the attacks happen east of this single building."

Peter crinkled his nose as he glanced at Cassie. "Lots of the killings in Cold Springs aren't too far from the Curios building," he said.

"Except the one's in Potter's Fork, if you've included those murders. But they don't fit your theory."

"We don't know exactly where the campers were located. Potter's Fork is at least twelve miles long."

Cassie shrugged. "I suppose."

She wasn't comfortable talking about a murderer. Somehow imagining an actual person capable of such brutal murders made her muscles tense. A bear, a sickly, territorial bear has been killing people. Not a person.

"I suspect the werewolf works at the Curios," Peter said. "Sorry, Cassie, it makes the most sense if they did. They get off their shift, their car is already parked, and they head out into the forest. Susie was killed in May, not long after the Curios opened for the season. If I'm right, this narrows down the suspect pool considerably."

"Are any of your coworkers from out of town?" Liam asked as he added the three victims of Potter's Fork to his notes.

Cassie glanced at his total of twenty-five victims in six months.

"Not that I know of," Cassie said. Her irritably manifested in her rosy cheeks, and she fought to force it down by sheer willpower.

"Is there anything suspicious about any of them? Strangely toned bodies or an uptick in cravings for meat on a monthly basis?" Peter asked. Both he and Liam peered at her, their eyes closing in, making her feel trapped.

"Well, in all honesty, it wouldn't surprise me if all of them turned into vicious, drooling monsters beneath the full moon. Kyle lusts after power, wanting to make a lot of money with the least amount of work possible. Maddie is moody and tries to act rebellious to cover how smart she is, but I suppose that would make her shifty." Cassie chuckled at the pun. She was amused by her comparisons, until her smile faded when mentioning Jeremy. "And then there's Jeremy. I overheard him talking to Maddie about how much he loved Susie and that if she was with him that night, she would still be alive."

Cassie figured Jeremy Rogers cared for Susie. It was no surprise. She noticed his lingering looks whenever

Susie and Peter came into the Curios. Susie liked the glass figurines of fairies. But it wasn't him. Peter would have known Jeremy all his life, Maddie too.

"Then there's Mr. Whittle who visits, off season, every other weekend," Cassie said. "They're weird people, but I don't think any of them are werewolves. There are no such things as werewolves. I know you've had a ton of time on your hands to obsess over that night, Peter. We all have experiences in our lives that haunt us, but the monster you're talking about doesn't exist.

"Now, I think we've taken this nonsense far enough. I'm sorry, Peter. I believe you described what you remember, but I've been in stressful situations before, and I know what fear does to a person. The human mind makes up false memories all the time. It tries to fill in the blanks of what it can't explain. There are no such things as werewolves." She turned to Liam. "And you are something else altogether. To hear you talk. It's as if it's a serial killer cosplaying a beast in some elaborate scheme. The killer would need to possess unbelievable skills of design, engineering, and not to mention speed and inhuman strength. This person doesn't exist. He definitely doesn't live in Cold Springs, or work at the Curios."

Liam and Peter sat silently, blinking in surprise from her words.

"I guess we could rule out the Curios," Peter said. "But there have been sightings of werewolves all over the country."

"Let me guess," Cassie said, a sly look washed over her face, "you found everything and anything about werewolves on the internet?"

Peter slid Liam back his phone. "Of course, I did. How else am I going to get my information when researching supernatural creatures?" he responded, half-joking, half-serious. "Most of them want to be rid of this curse because they're good people who don't want to kill, but they can't control it. And thanks to the internet, there was this guy in Oregon who vlogged about his experience of transforming into a werewolf. His name was Harvey, or something funny like that, you can look up his socials. Anyway. His body went through changes before his first transformation, getting all toned and his senses heightening. He noted how much he craved meat and how he used to wear glasses. He even showcased going to the eye doctor and getting a clean bill of health—20/20 vision when it was terrible vision the year before."

"So he went to gym and got Lasik, and went viral because of it," Cassie said dryly. "People lie all the time in order to get views or likes or just plain attention."

Peter's eyes narrowed. "I don't think he's like that."

Cassie took a deep breath to gather herself. "Peter, I'm so sorry about what happened to you and Susie. I really think you should see someone to help you make sense of everything and find some peace. There's no shame in getting help."

Peter fiddled with a fry. "I know what I saw."

Liam rested his napkin on the table. "Well, let's pretend you're right. Let's pretend the killer *is* a werewolf. What do you know about it?"

Cassie shot Liam a sharp look. She didn't think it was wise feeding into Peter's delusions, but the boy lit up as he started to explain. "Werewolves can't help but transform. It's a cyclical thing. I read all about it online. They possess a certain amount of energy which affects their supernatural abilities—super strength, great speed, and heightened senses. These ebb and flow with the cycle of the moon. They're the most human a few days surrounding a new moon, whereas they are the most powerful around a full moon. All that heightening energy needs to go somewhere and it builds until the body transforms, but it's gets crazier," he said as he straightened his back and took a sip of his water, "instead of transforming only once, the person transforms three nights in a row, regardless of the weather conditions. As long as the moon is full, they react to it through transformation. And in order to keep their energy levels high, they need to feed."

"So did my aunt whenever her blood sugar was low," Cassie said, throwing her hands up.

Liam's focused facial expression didn't shift. "Go on," he said. "Where do you think they'll be tonight?"

Peter picked up another fry, feeling justified by his interest. "I don't know. There are so many places they could go. Which is why I've decided to lure it to me."

"What?" Cassie asked. "Lure it to you?"

Peter motioned to Liam. "You saw the map, there are hundreds of miles the creature could cover. I tried to lure it to me last night, but it didn't work."

"Wait you were at the campsite?" Cassie's shoulders tensed. "And you didn't come forward with that information to the police?"

Peter shook his head. "I wasn't at the campsite. I was further north of the Curios. I wanted to lure the beast to me."

Liam slid his empty plate to the edge of the table. "Why? Regardless of what this thing is, why put yourself in danger?"

Peter looked around the serving area for prying eyes. When he suspected the coast was clear, he leaned in. "Because I intend to kill it. It's the only way."

Cassie's stomach soured at the thought of Peter hanging around after nightfall searching for a killer.

"And that's where I'm done," she said.

Cassie started sliding toward the edge of the booth, forcing Peter to stand to let her out. "I'm sorry, I can't become an accomplice to murder . . . or talks of killing people . . . or whatever we're talking about now. I've indulged enough on all these ridiculous theories and assumptions. I'll cover the bill and tip. It's been a pleasure knowing you Liam, you know your way to the town hall parking lot. Peter, get some help. Please."

Liam watched Cassie storm away toward the register. He regretted upsetting her. It was clear she was uncomfortable and worried about Peter. Though Peter sounded a bit insane, wasn't this the same conclusion

Liam was leaning into? What if he finds his killer and they try to kill him? He still hadn't figured out a solid plan, but perhaps Peter could play a part.

Liam motioned for Peter to sit.

Cindy approached the table and picked up the empty plates. "The cherry pie is almost out of season, so it's now or never. Could I interest you in a slice?"

Liam ordered two slices and turned his attention back to Peter. "What you are suggesting . . . " He searched for less offensive terms to spare Peter's feelings of insanity.

"It's the only way to stop a werewolf from killing more people," Peter said, as if the interruption had never happened. "You're so invested in finding this guy, what do you plan on doing once you find him?"

Liam's face softened. "Peter, again, there's no such things as werewolves. And what I intend to do isn't exactly what you're thinking."

Peter stared at Liam as if he'd stabbed him in the back. "The werewolf will transform again tonight. If I draw it to me and kill it, then no more deaths happen. Plain and simple. I may not know exactly where the beast will be tonight, could be the campgrounds, could be miles away from Cold Springs, but I know where they'll begin. Springs Meadow."

Peter motioned to see Liam's phone once again. He reluctantly obeyed, handing the boy his phone, and hoping it was the right thing to do.

Peter zoomed in on a blurry trail between Springs Meadow and Campsite #7. "There are hundreds of trails lining miles of ground, but three main trails lead from Springs Meadow all the way to Potter's Fork. Two of the three snake through Grover's Pike and one ends at the entrance of Camp Tree Trail."

He paused as Cindy dropped off the two slices of cherry pie and took the rest of the dishes.

Liam lifted his fork but wasn't as excited to eat all of the sudden.

Peter took a big bite of his pie before continuing. "Now, these trails join as one for a quarter of a mile between Springs Meadow and the border of Campsite #7 at Grover's Pike. This is where I plan on luring it. It's enclosed and I should get a good shot from any direction. Plus with everyone freaked out about last night, the trail will be completely empty."

Liam stared at the clearing. "How can you be certain your plan would work? You said you tried it out last night. You're still alive."

"Because the others were louder than me.

Werewolves have exceptionally good hearing. I plan on being the nosiest thing out there."

Returning his view to the clearing, if Peter was right, then perhaps the killer could see him as an easy target. If Liam used Peter as bait . . . No that would be wrong.

"You sound so sure about this werewolf," Liam said.

"Because these creatures are driven by instinct. They can't help it. Death is the only way to relieve these people from their affliction. There's no cure for being a werewolf. There's no way of controlling it either. This is why every movie and every book about werewolves ends in them getting shot, decapitated, or burned to death."

Liam took back his phone and stared at Peter. Is this what he looks like to others whenever he talks about a serial killer? Is this the mirror he needed to see, realizing how obsession changes a man?

He let out a long, drawn breath as he considered why Peter wanted to stop the killer. "I'm going to be honest with you, Peter. I know what it's like to lose someone, so I know how much you want to get this thing. But please let me handle this. I don't want you spending your best years in jail for murder."

"Because you assume it's a man I'd be killing. He's not human anymore." Peter poked the air with his fork to make a point. "I know it sounds crazy, but I'm not giving up. I'm heading to that clearing tonight. You can join me if you want, but you're not stopping me. I'm going to kill a monster."

Liam's face paled as he realized the depth of Peter's determination. "How are you going lure him to you?" His question was purely out of curiosity. He was past the point of judgement as he thought about the shotgun in his trunk.

Peter slid his empty plate aside. "An elk caller, actually, and the moment I look into its bright orange eyes, I'm going to kill it. They're weakest against silver. But the point is, he's going to transform again tonight, and I'm going to be ready."

Peter slid out from the booth.

"Is there any way of talking you out of this?" Liam asked.

Peter stood in the aisle. "What kind of person would I be if I let more people die when I could prevent it?"

Liam watched him walk away. He considered going after the boy, but he'd been in Peter's shoes and knew there was no deterring him. He also didn't want to attend another press conference tomorrow reporting Peter's death. The grieving boy taking matters into his own hands complicated things, but he'd also given Liam an incredible lead. Without Peter, Liam would be wandering around the forest all night hoping to stumble upon some rebellious and unfortunate campers, and now he had what he needed to end this tonight. He just wished he didn't have to look out for Peter while pursuing a killer.

Sitting in a booth and tapping his pen, Deputy Dustin King attentively looked over his notes. The pad and pen were inseparable for the forty-something, and he always jotted a thought or two among its pages. Between the faded blue lines, he'd recorded details of the strange conversation he'd eavesdropped on.

"Werewolf," the deputy whispered. "Campsite #7." His faded gray eyes lingered on the location Peter intended to occupy that night. King tapped his pen against the paper, wondering what to think of it.

"Would you care for a dessert Deputy?" Cindy asked, holding her own pen and notepad.

He didn't look away from his notes and nodded in response. "Peach pie with extra whipped topping, please." He turned back a page.

"Excellent choice," Cindy said and tucked her pad and pen into a large pocket. "Coming right up."

Deputy King studied the shorthand notes relaying Peter's true intentions. Normally, he'd pay little attention to what the strange boy would have to say. Folks who knew Peter understood he was traumatized by the attack, but King always wondered if there was some truth behind Peter's experience.

The young man's descriptions of the creature hadn't changed. His story was the same. The deputy had been around many people claiming outrageous things. Mrs. Parker claimed a slime monster lived in her bathroom sink, and Tally Windle believed he was abducted by aliens. But each time King would randomly bring up the strange claims, asking for updates on the matters, both Mrs. Parker and Tally would change a little detail about their stories. The slime monster would be brown instead of green and the alien ship was suddenly hexagonal instead of triangular. But Peter's claim about the werewolf hadn't changed.

The deputy clicked his pen as he debated on whether to report his findings to Sheriff Rhoades. He didn't think the old man would care for Peter's supernatural assumptions and wouldn't be surprised by the out-of-towner tagging along to enable his delusion further.

Cindy returned and set the piece of peach pie on the tabletop, her bangs bouncing with each turn of her head.

"There you go," she said.

"Thank you," the deputy replied. He circled the words *Campsite #7* before digging into his pie.

SEVEN

Parking at the Cold Springs Hubby Hole, Liam turned off the car and sat for a moment in the air-conditioned cab. He couldn't stop Peter from luring the murderer out from hiding, but Liam still felt like he was using the boy as bait and putting him in danger.

He didn't want to think too much about it. If he allowed himself to be too honest, he might realize that, even with his trunkful of gear and months of planning, he was confronting this evil prematurely. He should take more time and exert more control over the situation. But he couldn't back out now. Not when he knew Peter's plan.

Ever since Peter had uttered the word *werewolf*, Liam had tried to steer the boy away from the theory. The boy was going to get himself killed, and Liam saw enough of his own determination in Peter to know nothing short of death could stop him from pursuing this lead. Like it or not, he had a partner on this hunt.

Liam opened the door, allowing a wave of heat to infiltrate the car. He walked up the stairs to his motel room, glancing at the car one last time. The contents of his trunk reminded him what needed to be done.

A couple took their time unlocking their door as they kept distracting one another with giggles and kisses.

Liam ignored them as he stepped into his room. They must have been newlyweds. He'd been that happy once, but he couldn't remember what it felt like.

Liam closed and bolted the door, his thoughts racing like a thousand wild thoroughbreds.

A werewolf. The boy thought he saw a werewolf. What lingered in Liam's mind was Peter's thirst for revenge, even as he claimed a werewolf couldn't control itself. Liam understood what it was like to be driven by circumstances he couldn't control. In this regard, he and Peter were no different than the killer, or the criminal teenagers Liam had worked with. Liam still believed the choices people made within their circumstances were the defining factor. Putting more evil into the world was never the answer, and there was always another way.

Liam also believed in consequences for choosing

evil, but he wanted them to come through correct channels. Murdering the killer would be an act of evil. If only he could catch the guy and put him into the correct channels so he could get the help he needed. Deadly force would be a last resort of self-defense, not the primary goal.

This is where he and Cassie came to an agreement. Losing Leslie and Ruth taught him just how precious life was, and he wouldn't destroy a life when an alternative existed.

Humidity coated his skin, prompting him to turn on the air conditioner. The temporary interruption brought little relief as exhaustion set in from his restless night and mental strain of the day.

He laid back on the bed, squeezing his eyes shut. He heard similar assumptions and expressions months after Leslie and Ruth's passing, from a man not much older than Peter. The words of hopelessness echoed from the deep grooves of his brain. He wanted to shut it off. Change the channel. But as he lay with his fingers interlocked over his stomach, Liam steadied his breath, focusing on the rise and fall of his hands with each inhale and exhale.

"They can't help it," Peter's voice echoed in his

mind. *"They can't help it."* The words repeated like the caught needle on a vinyl record.

"I can't help it," another familiar voice spoke.

Liam turned to his side and hugged his knees. "Don't think about it Liam, she wouldn't want you to dwell."

But the memory poured over him like a mist creeping along the floor and filling the room.

It was six months after Leslie and Ruth's death. Liam had recovered from his injuries and sold their house in Augusta, Maine. He bought a cabin on the outskirts of Blood Moon, Pennsylvania. It was there he tried to live a normal life.

A little after midnight, Liam rests his head upon his pillow and listens to the wind strike against the window. Lightning rips through the dark clouds, thunder booming in its wake as a snowstorm slowly rolls into the valley. The beautiful moon hangs in the sky like a flickering bulb with storm clouds crawling across its face. Liam tries to relax amid the natural chaos when a loud bang sounds at the front door.

The bang repeats constantly. Whoever is at the door intends to wake Liam at all costs.

"I'm coming," he says as he rushes down the stairs, half irritated and a little fearful. Nobody has ever

bothered him at such an hour, which makes him nervous to answer the door. Was this someone who desperately needed help, or was it something more sinister?

The heavy fisted knock shakes the door as Liam pulls it open, revealing a man in his early twenties. The man backs away off the porch, putting a good distance between them. He is soaked through from the wet snow. His mop of red hair clings to his cheeks and neck, and he breathes as though he's just finished a marathon. His shoulders rise and fall with each gulp of air.

"Can I help you?" Liam asks.

The man speaks with a raspy tenor voice, pained, and tormented. "I'm so sorry for what I did. I needed to find you. I needed you to know how much I wish . . . I wish I hadn't—" He struggles to speak as his tears mix with the icy flakes on his cheeks. "I was trying so hard—so hard to fight the urges, but I couldn't help it. I—I can't help it." He pounds his chest like an ape and stomps his foot. "My uncle didn't think it'd be a problem for me to hang out at his cabin, that weekend." The younger man then hits the sides of his head as if to dump the memory out through his ears. "I killed him too. Slit his throat wide open. I didn't want to stop. It felt good to just give in, you know? It always does."

Is this really him? The man who killed Leslie and Ruth? Liam's first instinct is to beat the man senseless, but the stranger appears genuinely distressed.

The man paces the ground mixing the mud and freshly falling snow. He scratches his forehead furiously. "I'm so sorry for everything. I wanted to tell you as soon as you got out of the hospital but I was a bit detained at the time. What I did to your family . . . what I did to you . . . I'm a horrible person. A terrible, terrible person."

Liam keeps his rage secured within his tight fists and steps onto the porch to get a better look at his visitor.

The man stomps his foot again and paces nervously as his hands trembled. Liam has seen a few teens in a similarly delirious state when they were picked up off the streets. The nervous twitch, the bloodshot eyes, the constant shaking hands might be a bad trip or withdrawal of an addict. Liam mentally lists the possible drugs the guy could be on.

"The tent. The green tent," the man says. He wrings his hands as if to clean them. "And the little pink sleeping bag. The small teddy bear." He looks into Liam's green eyes. "They never caught me," the man says with a half-smile, but it bears more pain than pleasure. "I was just too fast when I heard the gunshots."

Liam looks around, making sure the man came alone. He forces his rage to a dark pit in his stomach as he focuses on getting the man out of the cold.

"Who are you? What's your name?" Liam steps off the edge of his porch and into a thin layer of wet snow accumulating at his bare feet.

The man stops pacing and faces Liam. He twitches as if his wiring had shorted.

"I don't want to go inside and talk, it's only a matter of time . . . when." He stops and cracks his neck. "My name is Benjamin Baird. I killed your wife and child and left you for dead. I couldn't help myself. I tried to go where I wouldn't hurt anyone."

Benjamin pinches his arm as if to keep focus on his words, which sound rehearsed. "I'd seen her out for a morning walk, your daughter. I liked how the light struck her hair. I couldn't stop wondering what it would be like to . . ." He pinches himself again.

"There's something wrong with me," he says with a cold look in his eyes. His lips twitch as he grinds his teeth. "Something terrible that I can't control. Something seductive and haunting. Sometimes I don't want to control. It feels ... so ... good."

Liam shakes his head. "There's nothing wrong with

you. I know exactly what you mean, and there's nothing wrong with you." The lie burns like bile in his mouth, but he's willing to say anything in order to get Benjamin into the house.

But Benjamin doesn't move. His dark eyes penetrate Liam's gaze. "So you've felt it too? You hear the voices?"

Liam doesn't know how to respond. He stands like an actor who has forgotten their lines.

Benjamin continues. "So you know that there is something terribly wrong with me. I shouldn't enjoy the thrill, the rush. It's not normal."

A surge of mixed emotions zip through Liam's veins. To hear the man's perverted indulgences, makes every muscle in his body tense with an urgency to fight. Thunder rumbles nearby, almost as though Liam's frustration has found a voice.

This is the guy who has eluded the police for months. If only Liam can have a chance to talk with him.

"I've done so many terrible things," Benjamin says. "I can't help myself. I feel like two people in one body. One wants to keep searching for the next victim, but the other wants to just end it all. I don't know who the real person is anymore."

Mud crusts Liam's cold feet as he approaches

Benjamin with outstretched arms and open hands. "It's alright," he repeats, in a soft tone. "I'm sure we can talk more about this inside. I can help you—"

"I didn't stop after your family, you know. So many people have died because of me. Their bodies will never be found." He lets out a chuckle. "There really wouldn't be much left."

Liam keeps his body and face calm, hiding his true emotions boiling beneath the surface.

"Let me help you," he says one last time.

Benjamin steps away from Liam. "Nobody can help me. I try to resist, but the voice in my head doesn't stop." He taps his head with his fingertips. "It doesn't shut up. I'm tired. I'm tired of fighting its pull. You're the only who's ever survived. That's why I needed to find you, to tell you I'm sorry. There's no hope for me. There's no hope for anyone." He pauses and showcases a dark look. "Not even for you."

Benjamin reaches into the back of his waistband and pulls out a gun. Liam holds up his hands, an instinctive but futile gesture. Why did he leave the safety of his cabin? Benjamin has come to finish what he started.

Liam's feet slip as he tries to sprint back into the house.

A gunshot tears through the wind and thunder, and Liam cries out, bracing for the sharp impact and searing pain, but nothing comes. He has no time to celebrate his luck that Benjamin is a poor shot. He reaches the door, slamming it shut behind him.

Benjamin hasn't fired a second shot. Why not?

Liam races to the window and peers outside.

Blood fills the muddy footprints surrounding Benjamin's fallen body, steaming in the cold night air.

EIGHT

treams of light broke between branches of the evening trees, touching the ground in filtered plumes of mist. Crickets chirped quiet songs as forest animals stirred in their sleep or leapt here and there on their nocturne journey through tall aspen and oak trees.

Peter stood among the serene calm, fiddling with an elk caller between his fingers. He'd practiced the elk bugling for weeks, trying to get the right pitch and volume. From accounts he'd read, only the werewolf's instinct to replenish its energy was the strongest pull toward its bloodlust. If he sounded like a suitable prey, such as an elk, he figured the werewolf would have no choice but heed the call and attack. He'd also avoid attention from authorities, when using the elk call. He'd blend in with the other natural sounds of the forest. So long as no one saw his car parked deep in the forest, he shouldn't be discovered.

Placing the call behind his teeth, Peter gently nestled it against the roof of his mouth. A film of latex rested on his tongue. He lifted a camouflaged tube, shaped like a bottle with the bottom cut out, and pressed it against his mouth. He squeezed his diaphragm and exhaled, allowing a flow of air to vibrate the latex skin and produce a high-pitched shriek which trumpeted into the night hoping to catch on wicked ears. A cry broke through the quiet evening, thrumbling in a rhythmic pulse until it dropped off.

Peter repeated the shrilly cry, hearing its echo in the distance, just as it happened the night before. The pitch rose to a high squeal then sank to a low hum.

"C'mon. Come find me," he said and pocketed the plastic piece. He hooked the bottle to his belt loop with a makeshift connecter of twine and a carabiner.

Then he waited.

In the pale light, he stood on the trail which connected the Curios to Campsite #7. Also attached to his hip was a holster, housing an automatic Glock 19 with homemade silver casted bullets. Using what knowledge he gleaned from the internet, Peter casted his bullets with the use of his cousin's welding tools and carbon rods. Melting down what crude silver coins and silverware he found from yard sales, he was able to pour the molting metal into clay casts. When set and cooled, he sanded, buffed, and polished each head, and carefully attached them to 9-millimeter casings. He created twelve rounds and while his uncle was away on a business trip, he took the Glock from its case. He knew what he did was dangerous and illegal, but it was the only way he could safely dispatch the evil which lurked in the shadows.

"I'm going to get this thing, Susie," he whispered. Peter often felt Susie nearby, so he'd taken to having one-sided conversations with her. Tonight, the thought of her presence watching over him made him feel less afraid of what he was about to confront. He still pictured her in her red Prom dress with shiny sequins sewn into the sheer skirt and bodice. She looked so beautiful.

Peter looked over his shoulder, realizing his back was to an open space. He'd stopped at the small clearing, his sneakers left prints in the soft dirt trail like an astronaut first stepping on the moon. Fewer trees grew in this location, but their tall trunks shaded him from the moon's light. From in between the rustling leaves, Peter spied the moon in all its glory, its brilliant white light almost blinding him.

In the distance, foliage snapped. Rustling came from the direction of the campsite and grew closer and closer. Something was approaching Peter a few steps at a time, as if it were trying to stay hidden, stalking him.

Peter pulled his gun free of it holster, its black steel body like a shadow in his hand. Maybe it was Liam, finally showing up after all, but it also might be the werewolf. His eyes darted in the direction of the approaching foe, and he aimed the gun, every muscle, as stiff as stone.

"Peter?" a familiar voice spoke from behind a tree. "It's Deputy King. I overheard your plans today at the diner."

A human hand reached into the air followed by a long arm covered in yellow plaid.

Peter lowered his gun. "Deputy King?"

Peter hadn't counted on anyone other than Liam possibly following him. Now Deputy King was going to find him trespassing, breaking curfew, and holding a gun he shouldn't be in possession of. He considered running, but he'd already sounded the elk call. The werewolf could be on his way.

Deputy Dustin King stepped from behind the tree. Except for the badge hanging around his neck, he wasn't in uniform, but instead wore a dark-yellow plaid shirt and blue jeans. His brown boots pushed aside the tall grasses as he approached with his hands slightly out to the side, palms raised to show they were empty. Peter figured he had a weapon concealed somewhere.

"I'm concerned about you Peter. I've come to try and reason with you."

"Concerned? Reason with me?" Peter repeated. "If you'd taken me serious in the first place, I wouldn't have to be out here right now."

"I'm not going to lie to you," King said. "You're not a minor anymore, and you're in a bit of trouble right now." He motioned to the gun. "If you hand over the weapon and come along with me, we can file this as a lapse in judgement instead of criminal intent."

"You need to leave," Peter said. The creature could show up any second. He didn't want the deputy involved or endangered, but if Peter didn't finish this tonight, he'd never get another chance. The police and his uncle would make sure of it.

King's face softened, an attempt to show the look of a wise old friend. "Peter, I know what you're going through, losing Susie and all. But this isn't the way to handle it."

"I know what I saw, and I don't want anyone else

getting killed. Now, something very dangerous is coming this way and you need to go. Your bullets won't stop it. Only I can stop it."

Keeping his hands in front of him, the deputy slowly stepped closer to the young man. "You were right. Everyone should have been more supportive, and I'm going to do better. I believe you have the best intentions, and I commend you for being so brave, but breaking the law and putting yourself in danger isn't the right way to resolve the problem. Let the officials handle this. It's what we're here for."

Peter holstered his gun, recognizing the nervous look on the deputy's face. "Some job you're doing. Too many people have died this summer, and it's not going to stop." Peter let out a frustrated sigh. "Unless I do something right now."

A howl echoed over the treetops like a bassoon's deep note held too long. The werewolf was close but not close enough. "Please, deputy, you need to leave," Peter said. "There isn't much time. You can arrest me tomorrow. Trust me, I'll happily turn myself in."

Even in the pale moonlight, Peter saw the blood drain from King's face as he took the last few steps to Peter's side. "You aren't equipped in stopping this thing all by yourself," King said. "Come with me. I can radio in and have five guys out here, armed, and capable of shooting anything that crosses their path."

"It wouldn't matter," Peter said between quick breaths. "They'd be too late." He raised his elk bugle once again and returned the call, rhythmically breathing his highest note before allowing it to deepen.

The crickets stopped chirping.

King drew his gun, concealed in his waistband, and his brow glistened with sweat as he frantically searched the area.

"C'mon Peter, we need to get out of here," King said nervously. "We're in danger. I don't want to go up against a bear right now."

"I'm not going anywhere!" Peter said. "It won't be long until the werewolf comes. You still have time to run."

King shook his head as he searched for a place to hide. Peter now held the Glock's handle securely in his hand and kept a steady stare in the direction of the howl.

"I'm not leaving without you, Peter. If anything terrible happened to you, I wouldn't forgive myself for not trying."

Peter shrugged, ignoring King's last attempt of

talking him into leaving. "Fine, but I wish you'd go. It's for your own safety."

Then, like the galloping of a horse, the sound of heavy bounding limbs broke through the silent night, matching the quick thuds of Peter's beating heart. King stood behind Peter, joining his anxious stare into the distance.

Wet, guttural breaths rose in a chorus of excitement. The beast dashed along the dark tree trunks, kicking up dirt and disturbing the foliage around it. Its long claws slashed at a trunk, giving it enough momentum to vault off the ground and into the treetops. It leapt nimbly from one tree to the next, easily catching the thick limbs and trunks with its claws.

"Peter—" King said between gasps of stunned horror.

"Do you believe me now?"

Both guns quivered in the air, fixed on a target that remained out of range. Like a first-person shooter game, Peter's arm swayed hard to the left following it, while King turned on his heels to get a clear shot. Peter stood steady, watching the trees jostle and jar.

"What's it doing?" King asked.

"I don't know." The beast should have charged

by now. This felt different than what Peter had seen at Springs Meadow and what others had described.

The werewolf dropped to the ground and hid in the shadow of a large aspen. Its orange eyes reflected what little light filtered through the branches. From its position, Peter could tell it crouched low to the grass like a cat ready to pounce. He wouldn't have a clear shot until it jumped.

The blood had already drained from Peter's arm, making his fingers numb and tingly. He switched hands but couldn't pull the trigger.

"Come on. Why aren't you charging?" he mumbled.

Crouched low to the trunk of the tree, the monster growled. Its shadowed eyelids narrowed, the glow from its eyes now horizontal slits, and it shrunk deeper into the darkness, almost vanishing entirely.

"Where did it go?" King asked.

The beast then sprang from its hiding place. Peter fired two quick shots that didn't land before the deputy grabbed his wrist, a silent warning to wait for a clear shot, as the monster climbed another tree and roared.

The deputy aimed, having his sights on the beast's chest, and fired. Within moments, the bullet soared through the air, missing its target and instead, lodging deep into the bark of the trunk. The beast maneuvered quickly out of its way and leapt to another tree high above them.

Peter regretted shooting, as his silver bullets were limited.

"Do you see it?" King asked.

Peter's knees knocked against one another as he frantically searched the darkness. His fear covered him like a thick blanket too impenetrable to break from. What was he thinking? This was too overwhelming and his instinctual need to run was winning against his need to fight.

"My gun," Peter said, extending his weapon for King to take. "It has silver bullets. You're a better shot than I am."

The deputy took a step in the direction of the campsite where he'd parked. "You keep it. We need to move!" But King's words were abruptly interrupted when the deep shadow dropped from the treetops and landed directly onto him. Peter leapt out of the way, screaming. He tripped backward and hit the ground with his shoulder, the impact tossing the gun into the long grass.

Amid the commotion of terrified screams and growls, the deputy struggled against the beast's hulking frame. The behemoth must have been at least eight feet tall and lumbered over the deputy, pinning him with one meaty hand.

King's frantic cries mingled with raspy barks and snarls. The smell of animal fur, dust, and sweat assaulted Peter's nostrils as the werewolf wrenched the gun from King's hand, snapping his wrist in half. The deputy yelled. The werewolf roared.

Peter anticipated the monster tearing into the man's body, but instead the beast swiped the back of its clawed hand across King's face, rendering him unconscious, perhaps dead, with a single blow.

Peter stared, frozen with uncontrollable fear. Flashes of the night Susan died struck him like lightning. The blood. The screams. Peter's body went completely numb as he stared in horror at the man-like creature slowly rising to the balls of its feet. Its orange eyes fixed on him as its large hands curled into fists. Hot breath heaved into the cool night air. Its long-bristled tail brushed the dirt off of King's boots as it let out a long and threatening growl.

Peter scrambled to where his gun had disappeared into the shadows, bracing for the monster's fierce attack. Peter rifled through the tall grasses, hoping to touch metal.

Something was off. The beast hadn't fed on the deputy, and it was sure taking its time attacking Peter. He shouted, too afraid to look over his shoulder as he kept grasping blades of grass.

The werewolf released another threatening growl, sending chills all over Peter's body. And then, like an answer to his terrified cries, Peter found the gun.

Spinning around, without thinking he fired. The bullet grazed the beast's shoulder, singeing the fur as it dug deep into a tree trunk. Peter fired again, this time hitting the creature in the forearm.

A menacing roar pierced the air, its deep bellow rattling Peter's ribs. He saw black claws scrape and dig a path of destruction where the bullet tore into the beast's arm. Sinews of flesh broke down as globs of blood and silver poured from the wound. A painful yelp burst from the beast as it wrenched its claws deeper into the mound of muscle and removed not only the bullet, but a handful of melted skin and tissue surrounding it.

Peter couldn't believe the effect of silver on the creature. He gathered himself to take aim again, but the werewolf took off into the forest in a flash of shadow and moonlight.

"No!" Peter shouted. He banged his fist against the ground.

Deputy King twitched and he slowly returned to consciousness.

Peter doublechecked to make sure the deputy was alright. "Still breathing," Peter said with relief.

He stood and with one last deep breath, his determination to fight returned with full force.

"You're going to be alright," he breathed, assuring himself more than anything, and he ran after the beast.

eter's heart banged against his ribcage as he chased after the werewolf, fueled by a mixture of rage and determination to kill. In the distance, the beast wove in between trees, bounded over brush, and slinked through thickets.

"No!" Peter shouted. "Stop!" The words exploded from him.

As he ran, Peter tried to steady his gun, but as soon as he had a clear shot the beast leapt out of view. The young man pumped his legs harder, the last of his adrenaline fueling each step. He left the path, the strip of security which guided him through the forest, and dodged low-hanging branches, thick patches of foliage at his feet and uneven ground. With a fixed gaze on the back of the beast, Peter tried again to stop his moving target.

Firing his sixth silver bullet, the projectile tore

through the beast's left ear and impacted the ground yards ahead, the silver disintegrated beneath specks of red blood. An angry roar cut through the night, as sharp as lightning and as deep as thunder. The beast took larger strides through the misty light, and Peter soon found himself in a rocky clearing at the foot of a mountain.

The boy searched his surroundings. He was well off of the familiar trails, but the mountain and roar of rushing water helped him orient himself. The clearing bore a lake of jagged rocks and fallen trees. A wildfire had scorched the area, leaving the skeletal remains of pine trees to mark the boundary between thriving life and complete desolation. The mountain looming above the clearing appeared split in two, as if God, himself, had struck it with an ax.

Peter's shoes struggled for purchase against the jagged rocks. The werewolf moved easily over the rough terrain a few yards ahead, surefooted.

This was Peter's chance. This was the moment he had to pull the trigger and stop the murderer. This moment which played in his mind for months. And yet.

And yet, there was something off about the whole situation.

His head cleared by the exertion of running, Peter

revisited what he'd seen. The werewolf didn't tear the deputy apart, and it hadn't come after him. The thought gnawed at him. Matthew Larsen had described how the creature had attacked his friends as brutally as it had attacked Susie, killing instantly.

His mind raced through all the articles he'd read about the emotional state of werewolves. He'd concluded that it was the nature of the beast to kill, not to spare. Could he have read partial truths?

As his belief of what constituted as an absolute about the supernatural creature slowly dissolved like sand sifting in the wind, something else slinked closer to him.

Peter steadied his trembling hand and watched the werewolf he'd tracked, move closer to the trees. He knew pulling the trigger was the right thing to do, but something in him hesitated. He needed to decide. Even though the beast had showed compassion in sparing his life, it was up to him to relieve the creature of its curse.

"This is for Susie," he whispered beneath his breath.

His finger curled around the trigger, applying the right amount of pressure to discharge the bullet. Just as he fired, Peter slammed into the sharp rocks, knocking his shot wide and dislodging the gun from his hand. He rolled onto his back and faced the enormous fangs of another werewolf.

Peter pushed against the beast's hairy arms. Its black, wet nostrils flared; its teeth glistened in the moonlight. He cried out, matching the beast's snarls and deep growls, trying to keep a broad distance between his neck and the sharp teeth which inched their way closer to his flesh. His arms weakened beneath the creature's heavy shoulders as it snapped at his throat, creating a push of wind against his skin.

Staring into the orange iridescent eyes, the only thing racing through his mind were thoughts of Susie. The glimmering sparkles of her red sequined dress colored his vision. Her dark chestnut curls falling over her shoulders, clouded his mind as he heard her melodic voice speak his name. Amid the flood of fear there was a moment of peace. Peter did his best to avenge her death. He knew if the deputy got away, he'd know the truth and continue Peter's quest in killing this thing. He hoped he would soon reunite with the girl of his dreams and keeper of his heart.

The werewolf grabbed at his hair, yanking his head aside. Its sour breath made Peter's eyes water. He dug his fingernails into the beast's tough skin, like pressing against hardened clay, and pushed with what strength remained in his arms. As the large jaws of death neared his throat, he cried out one last time.

"Help! Please, help!"

The drip of warm saliva found his skin and pooled at the base of his neck. The beast let out guttural bark and then yipped when the other werewolf bowled it over, knocking it away from Peter's trembling body.

Peter rolled to his side to watch the chaos unfold. Caught in a dangerous bearhug, the beasts roared and pushed each other. One was bigger than the other, a brute with the wounds inflicted upon it from Peter's gun. Besides the obvious wounds and height difference, both creatures were almost identical, with a thick, brown pelt and fiery orange eyes.

Peter took a deep breath. "How is this possible?"

Fur bristled over the beasts' broad shoulders as it attacked. They pummeled and jabbed their claws into each other's bodies, slicing the flesh, and responding with deep roars, making Peter's teeth rattle.

The shot was clear. Searching for his fallen gun, Peter saw it glowing in the moonlight among the dark rocks. He grabbed it, leaping out of the way when the smaller werewolf lunged at him. The brute grabbed it by the scruff of its neck and pulled it off course, as if it were protecting Peter.

As the fight played out, Peter noticed how the larger werewolf, the one that spared Deputy King, redirected the smaller werewolf and kept the fight away from him.

The brute lunged at its opponent, grabbing it by the throat, and lifting it high above the ground. It held tight to the wriggling creature; their eyes locked in a deadly staring contest.

The meaty hand with long, sharp claws tightened around the smaller werewolf's neck. A choked whimper broke from the helpless opponent, its eyes rolling to the back of its head. Holding his breath with anticipation, Peter watched the brute slam the smaller werewolf hard against the ground, knocking it out cold.

With gun in hand, the young man stepped into the moon's light and faced the victor. The beast remained standing, panting heavily from the brawl. Its orange eyes blazed like bonfires.

"Who are you?" Peter asked. The creature had protected him when it should have attacked. Now there were two werewolves. Nothing made sense.

He lifted the gun when the werewolf turned toward him. Both stared at one another as they tried to figure out their next move. The beast lowered its head and slinked away in submission.

Almost instantly, the monster twisted and contorted. The thick pelt retracted into the skin, human hair replacing it. The monstruous bones broke and fused back into their natural frame. The muscles shrunk, the skin grew taut, and Peter searched the man's features.

"Liam?" The word broke from his lips in a single breath.

Carefully, Liam Fredricks stood to his feet, his naked body covered in blood as his gashes, bite marks and bruises continued to heal. A stream of blood caked the left side of his head. The forearm wound from Peter's bullet looked different from the others. The gash marks where Liam had dug out the bullet healed visibly, but the bullet hole still gaped.

Liam raised his good arm in surrender. "You wouldn't shoot unarmed man, would you?"

Peter paused not knowing what to say. "Are you sure you are a man?" he asked.

Glancing at the unconscious werewolf, Liam shrugged. "I suppose that's for you to decide. You have the gun."

Liam stepped away from Peter, taking his time walking over the jagged rocks with his clumsy human feet. Peter followed, gun still in his hand, but at his side.

"You can't be the killer," Peter said, his expression betraying his hope that he was right.

"I'm not the killer," Liam assured him. He entered a nearby thicket where he'd left his car. A little after sunset, Liam had parked and placed fresh clothes on the hood before transforming. He'd searched near Campsite #7 until he'd heard Peter's elk call. The police officer shooting at him had been a surprise. Liam hoped the deputy's injuries would heal completely.

Luckily for Liam, Peter wasn't as great of a shot. Though the deputy's bullets wouldn't have made much of an impact, had he hit him, the silver bullets would have easily sliced through his flesh like a hot knife slicing through butter. He'd dealt with silver before, years ago when he was first figuring out his new form, when he helped a neighbor set a table. Upon touching a silver spoon, Liam's skin blistered. He chalked it up as an allergic reaction but the moment Peter's silver bullet made contact, the searing pain was almost unbearable. The wound continued to burn as his body flushed out the tiny particles from his blood and muscle tissue.

"If you're not the killer, then that other one is." Peter tightened his grip on the gun and looked over his shoulder toward the unconscious creature. He glanced at Liam again, who could almost see the vengeful thoughts racing through the young man's mind. Peter didn't need to be a good shot to kill a still target, and Liam was too weak to stop him.

"Peter, wait! You're not a killer, either."

"I can't let it live after what it's done."

Satisfied that the boy wasn't about to dart away, Liam slipped on his black boxer briefs while saying, "I know, but you can let me get him as far away from Cold Springs as possible. I suspected the murderer was just like me. You've read how difficult it is to control this, but I've done it. I've managed to control the beast and I believe I can help others, others like me, do the same. I can save this werewolf's life and prevent more attacks."

Peter scoffed. "You sound just like Cassie. It won't work. It's in your nature."

"You believe everything you read online?"

Zipping up his jeans, Liam stepped into his sneakers.

He opened the front door and pressed a button to open the trunk. He paused to look at Peter's bewildered face. "I'm sorry I lied to you, Peter. It was the only way to avoid more questions and concerns you would have had about werewolves. I really didn't want anyone else involved in this."

Liam grabbed his shirt and moved toward the trunk, slipping it on as he walked.

Peter kept his distance from Liam. "Is there some secret society of werewolves? Some hierarchy you all follow? Are you an alpha?"

Liam searched the trunk for his rope, an involuntary smile forming on his lips about how quickly Peter had proven him right about the werewolf questions. "No. Not that I'm aware of. You probably know more than I do. I've just figured things out for myself with each passing month." Liam moved quickly as he spoke, uncertain how long the murderer would remain unconscious. He needed to tie him up as soon as he could.

Moving aside the heavy net, Liam found the rope, leaving the shotgun nestled beside tent stakes and a bat. He'd tested out various bullets, all proving ineffective, with the help from an old friend back in Blood Moon, but had yet to discover what a shotgun shell could do.

"So did the effects of silver match up with your research?" Liam asked, closing the trunk.

Peter didn't answer.

"Peter?" Liam called again, his heart beating a little faster.

Peter was gone.

Liam sprinted to the clearing. A shot was fired followed by Peter's yell.

With superior traction, the werewolf had dodged the boy's last effort of execution and held him in a deadly embrace. Peter had dropped the gun, his back now pressed against the creature's chest.

Liam watched helplessly as the werewolf sunk its teeth into the boy's neck.

"No!" Liam said to the werewolf. "Let him go. I know you understand me. You're in there, you can hear me."

The creature dug its fangs deeper into Peter's flesh, blood gushing from the bite, soaking his clothes in crimson tendrils.

Peter's hands and feet twitched as they dangled above the ground.

"Please don't." Liam slowly lowered the rope, it would be of no use now.

Opening its claws, the beast dropped Peter. The young man lay barely conscious on the ground, blood pouring from his mouth and the deep gash in the crook of his neck.

Guarding its prey, the killer revealed bloodied fangs. He placed a large, clawed hand on the young man's chest and pressed against his ribs. Liam heard popping noises as they cracked.

"Stop!" Liam demanded. Peter barely flinched. He needed medical attention, but Liam feared he'd already crossed the point of no return. He would either die of his injuries or survive as a werewolf, and Liam didn't know which was worse.

Liam weighed his options. He didn't have the energy to transform again, and the werewolf had dropped Peter on top of his gun with the silver bullets.

Liam stepped closer, prompting the beast to roar, forcing him to take a step back.

"Get away from him," Liam said. He met the beast's gaze and held it. "Back away now!"

He'd only encountered two other werewolves since his attack two years ago. Neither lived long enough to show him how to cope with the burdensome affliction. After his first transformation, a month after the attack, he thought only of Leslie as the next moon approached. It was remembering his human life which kept his humanity intact. Perhaps it would work with this beast.

Searching for a jolt of assertiveness, Liam swallowed a deep gulp of air, puffed out his chest, and released a roar. "Get away from him!"

The werewolf studied him but didn't move. Liam spread his stance and threw his shoulders back to make himself appear more intimidating, though he was sure he looked like an idiot to the beast.

"Get away from him!" he shouted again. A rumble reverberated in his chest and throat, giving him a familiar feeling of power. For over a year he'd managed to maintain a balance between his beast and human self. The deep demand he expressed gave him goosebumps, and made his eyes shine their iridescent orange.

The werewolf's ears turned back, and it gave a low growl of protest. It sniffed at him.

"You know exactly what I am. You can control this." Liam growled.

The beast submitted, turning its gaze to the ground.

"Think of your human form," Liam insisted, his voice more human than monster. "Remember what you look like. Picture your form, your hands, your face, your feet. Feel the sensation of moving your limbs and joints."

The two remained silent, their eyes fixed upon one another. Liam wasn't sure if his words were getting through to the human within. He patiently waited, still holding his dominating stance.

The werewolf started to pant heavily. Liam recognized the effort of transforming before the beast willingly subsided.

"That's right. Stay focused."

Without breaking his stare, and with the strict encouragement of a drill sergeant, Liam continued ordering the werewolf to remember who he once was.

He began with the physical sensations like tasting a good steak or feeling the touch of a lover's hand. Though it sounded a little silly, Liam was as serious as a pastor spouting sermons about the end of days. With each passing word, the beast would shudder and crumple as his body returned to its original form.

"Remember! Remember who you truly are."

The beast's panting slowed as he completed his transformation back into his human form, revealing the Cold Springs killer.

"It can't be," Liam gasped.

The Cold Springs killer.

The killer he'd been tracking since February was none other than Cassie Westbrook.

hat's why you look so familiar," Liam said, his shadow towering over Cassie's naked body. "In February, in Oxford, Maine. The apartment slaughter. I remember reading how there were five people murdered."

He looked at Cassie, who had her face buried in her hands. Liam pulled off his shirt and tossed it to her. She didn't look at him as she held it to her chest.

"There was one survivor," he said.

He remembered the moment he first saw her. Her face was much thinner than the old, black and white driver's license photo, and she'd bleached her brown hair blonde.

"But it wasn't a Cassandra Westbrook." He kept an attentive stare on her sullen blue eyes. The eyes that magnified the moonlight with her tears. "It was Evangeline Jones."

Cassie shuddered. "The last time anyone called me that, I was visiting my brother in New Hampshire trying to find a cure for this. He'd found a woman in Massachusetts claiming to know all things supernatural, but I transformed at the bus stop on our way out of town." Cassie pursed her trembling lips together and swallowed hard, fighting an overwhelming wave of grief.

"I'll get you more to wear." Liam walked briskly to his car, giving her some space.

He glanced at Peter, who's eyes stared blankly into the night, his chest lay still. He paused to listen for a heartbeat but the forest ambiance covered any proof of life. Liam didn't know what to feel, and he sighed, relieving the immense burden of sorrow and relief with his breath.

"I'm so sorry," he whispered.

He returned with a pair of gray sweats and slippers, backup clothes in case he ever ruined his during a transformation. He offered them to Cassie, hoping she'd accept. As he bent down to make sure she was alright, he remembered an Evangeline Jones had gone missing after the bus stop incident.

According to Liam's research, Evangeline was the sole survivor who gave details about a man in a puffy coat after he brutally attacked five people in her apartment. He didn't make the connection immediately that she could have been the werewolf. She later became a missing person when she disappeared after the bus stop incident. Since there was no DNA evidence, or eyewitnesses, linking her to the deaths of the three people, her brother included, she was presumed a victim herself and the case went cold.

"I didn't mean to kill anyone," Cassie said with a weak and raspy voice. "I loved my brother, my friends"—she choked back a sob—"my fiancé."

The victims closest to her.

The first people she killed.

"I'm sorry Evangeline—"

"Don't call me that," she snapped. "It's Cassie now. It has been ever since I went to Massachusetts, hoping to find relief. My brother had found a woman there, who claimed she could help, but it was all a scam to steal identities. Instead of moving on, I had her give me a new identity. Evangeline Jones is no more."

Her tears fell, making clean trails through the blood and dirt on her cheeks. "You came to Cold Springs to kill me. Do it. I deserve it."

"You've killed a lot of people," Liam said, his

offering still extended. "But killing you isn't why I'm here."

Her mouth contorted into a crooked smile. "What is wrong with you?" Cassie shivered in the cool night air. Within the moon's light, Liam watched her injuries heal. Deep gashes and cuts sealed themselves like zipping sandwich bags. Her bruises faded into creamy white skin. Her long blonde hair was caked in soot, dirt, and blood.

"I honestly wasn't sure what I was doing. The patterns all led to someone like me, but I was prepared if they turned out to be a true serial killer. Luckily, Peter's determination inspired me to decide."

Cassie's hand flew to her mouth. "Peter!" She glanced at the still body. "I did that. I didn't want to. I fought so hard to stop it." Cassie spoke no louder than a whisper. "For months I searched for a cure, but nothing worked. Tonight, I took three times the recommended dose of sleeping pills, and when I woke up, I was already transformed and out here. I don't want keep killing. I already have so much blood on my hands."

Kneeling on the rocks, Liam rested the clothes beside Cassie. "That's why I'm here. I can teach you how to control the beast within."

"You honestly think you can help me?" Cassie asked, her eyes burned with frustration.

Liam nodded. "Yes. I'm living proof that werewolves can control themselves."

Blood splattered and bruised, Cassie looked at the clothes and cried. "You should kill me. I won't fight you."

"Cassie, I'm not going to kill you."

Liam watched as overwhelming feelings of guilt, shame, and grief washed over her like a dam bursting from immense pressure. She hid her face in a mop of filthy hair and hugged her knees. He reached out, softly caressing her bare shoulder with his fingertips. She didn't flinch from his touch. Instead, she had leaned closer.

"I want to die," she said, as Liam wrapped his arms around her. "Not just because of what I've done, but because of what I am. I see all their faces through the beast's eyes. Every kill, every cry . . . I experience it too. I've done unforgivable things. Come the following moon, I'll only kill again. I can't control the beast."

Liam moved to look into her eyes. He brushed strands of hair from off her face. "I have a cabin in Blood Moon where I intend to teach you everything I know. Everything I've learned so far, I want to share that with you. We can leave Cold Springs as soon as things settle here. The deputy was with Peter and that may complicate things, but we can go to Blood Moon. It's just as secluded."

Silence bridged the gap between them as Cassie glanced at the clothes once again. She touched the soft fabric with her dirty fingertips. Blood and dirt clung beneath her nails and filled in the creases of her fingers. She paused to touch the backs of her hands, creating shadows on her skin.

"Can you tell me how it's possible that I'm human right now? Normally I don't shift back until the sun's up. How did you do what you did, forcing me back into my human form?" she asked. "I felt trapped in the beast's body, never capable of taking complete control."

"I call it the Calling because I call myself back to human. You picked it up quickly," Liam said. "You really wanted to be human. That says a lot about who you truly are."

Cassie handed Liam back his shirt as she slipped the sweater over her torso. "Who I truly am? I'm the person responsible for your whole list of murders." She stood and pulled on the sweatpants.

Liam averted his eyes, giving her privacy. "I'm

sorry for your loss. I could only imagine how it would feel to be responsible for the death of a family member, let alone a stranger."

Cassie pulled the drawstring on the sweatpants so forcefully that Liam could hear the string against the fabric. "I stayed in Amherst, Massachusetts because I had nowhere else to go. I thought Puffer's Pond would be a good place to transform, but four teens were way out in the middle of nowhere messing around. People are everywhere these days."

"Is this why you stayed in Cold Springs? The seclusion?"

Cassie put on the slippers and clapped her hands at her sides. "That, and I got tired of running. I had a life, Liam. I had a great job working as a freelance columnist for the local paper. I was going to marry my best friend. We were going to grow old together. Kurtis was a big-time fisherman. We'd go all over the country fishing. It worked out since I could email my work from anywhere, as long as I had access to the internet." A deep frown washed over her beautiful face. "But that night in January, we were ice fishing when that thing attacked. I would have died had Kurt not broken the ice, forcing the beast to sink into the cold water. He suffered minor scratches, but I wasn't so lucky. I don't know if my attacker survived or not. But I wish I hadn't."

"With practice it will become easier to handle this affliction." Liam stood and dusted off his jeans.

"Transforming back into my human form was just as painful," Cassie said. "I would have given up if you hadn't kept pushing me to keep going. How did you figure it out?"

Liam shrugged. "I don't know. I guess I needed the right motivation and didn't want to end up like the guy who attacked me and killed my wife and daughter."

Cassie gasped. "That's how you lost them?" She pressed her fingers to her mouth. "I'm so sorry."

Liam nodded. It's a horrific way to die. "It was two years ago. I survived the attack. I used to think Benjamin, my attacker, would have killed me if my brother hadn't shot him several times, but regular bullets are impervious to werewolf flesh. You still feel the impact, but unless you take a bullet to the eye or down the throat, they just hurt. Now I'd like to think Benjamin managed to break through the beast that night, finding his humanity—even for a moment—and sparing my life."

"Benjamin?" Cassie asked.

"He found me six months after the attack. When

I first saw him, I wanted to kill him for what he did, but there was a part of me that understood his pain. He confessed and took his own life. It was the moment I figured out the effect of silver on a werewolf's body. Though he was human when he shot himself, his wound was horrifying to say the least. By that time in my life, I'd already managed to control my transformations. But before then, I'd usually transform the exact time of my attack, 2:27 AM."

Cassie held up a hand to stop him. "Mine's 11:34 PM. I wondered if there was a connection."

"Yeah, well, most people aren't checking the time while being mauled to death." This prompted a stern look from Cassie, as if she sensed the insensitivity in the statement.

"Maybe if Benjamin had a stronger support system in place, or somebody to talk to, maybe all that death could have been prevented," Liam said. "Maybe I'd be a boring youth counselor with imposter syndrome in Maine right now, changing my second kid's diaper while Ruth plays dress up with Leslie."

Liam's voice fizzled as he glanced at Peter. "It's too late for Peter, but it's not too late for you. We should leave, now."

"We can't just leave him out here."

"He's already dead or will be in a matter of time. I can't hear his heart beating and he's not breathing."

Cassie reluctantly walked in the direction of the car. "There must be another way."

Liam escorted her around Peter's body. "There isn't, Cassie, and it's best that he dies. I don't know how it was for you," he said, "but that first month was hell."

He stepped onto lush green grass, passing a dead tree. Cassie followed like a child wanting to remain put.

"I came in and out of reality," Liam said. "I had nightmares, hallucinations. My body was healthy and healed within the first week, but I couldn't stay conscious for more than a few hours and hardly kept any food or fluids down. By the morning of the next full moon, I woke as if nothing had happened. My brother, Danny, took me home, and watched over me. I took it easy during the day but felt groggy."

"Like you'd woken up from a hangover," Cassie said.

"Yeah. Luckily for Danny, I didn't transform in the house. I remember waking and feeling drawn toward the moon. I remember staring at it. Feeling its light on my skin. I was at a soccer field when I finally made the shift.

I never really considered myself religious, but at that moment, God was the only thing I screamed out to."

Liam took in a deep breath and calmed his racing heart. Every time he recalled the memories his anxiety levels soared. "Thankfully the only blood that was spilt that night were of a couple neighborhood dogs."

Cassie wished that were her case. "The night I came home from the hospital, my best friend, Cassie Pearson, had thrown a little welcome-home party, keeping it simple with a few friends."

"Where was your family?" Liam asked.

Cassie stepped closer to the car. "My parents had died a few years ago in a car accident, leaving only my brother and me. I was living with Kurtis and we were intending to get married as soon as he put a down payment on a house. He was among those who I killed that first night."

She took a deep breath and held onto the car for support. "I remember resting on the couch, as Cassie's boyfriend, Gary Westbrook, debated if Almond milk should really be called milk." She chuckled at the memory but only half-heartedly, "I sometimes miss his random musings about dumb things like that."

Cassie glanced in Peter's direction. "There's a voice

in my head. I can drown it out, most of the time, but whenever the moon's full, it's louder than ever."

"I wish I could say it goes away," Liam said somberly. "I've managed to quiet it, but if it's not the voice, it's the memories. Always the memories."

Liam opened the door and motioned for Cassie to enter. In the pale, orange car light Cassie stood. "Tonight when I realized where I was and what form I was in, the beast wanted to finish what it started back in May. It intended to kill Peter."

Liam had remembered the tree trunk at Springs Meadow. "Those were your claw marks on the tree, weren't they?"

Cassie nodded and got into the car.

Taking one last glance at the bright full moon, Liam joined Cassie in the car and turned the ignition. He listened to her describe the night she killed Susan Eckert. The claw marks were a result of Cassie taking complete control for only a few moments, demanding the beast turn away, literally clinging to the tree in order to stop it.

"I couldn't hold it for long," she said. "I was surprised I was controlling the arm to begin with. I concentrated on not using the hand to kill. I dug my claws in deep, but the beast took over once again and pushed away, leaving the marks."

Liam had glanced at the side of the street, hoping to find Cassie's car but couldn't find it. "Cassie, did you run all the way out here?"

She shrugged, reminding him of the drugged-out state she was once under. "I'm not surprised if I did. I can cover a lot of ground." She placed her hands in her lap and fiddled with the grime beneath her nails. "I should turn myself in."

Liam sped toward Cold Springs, taking the same road that brought him here the night before. "I know it might feel wrong to be leaving all this behind. I can't determine where the beast ends and the human begins, and I'm definitely not in a position to morally judge, but how could you prove it? I guess you could transform in front of the press to show what you've become. But the beast has its own DNA sequences and finger pads. There's nothing human about us when in that form. Sure, you'd probably be committed to an asylum, but it wouldn't do much. And think about what could happen if you did transform to the public."

She folded her arms and sat silently. Liam could tell the wheels were turning as she rubbed her lips and sighed. "We shouldn't have left Peter behind."

Guilt coursed through Liam's veins. He couldn't go back for the boy. He couldn't have any connection to Peter's whereabouts. To help him would only bring more questions, and that was somehting Liam couldn't deal with.

"Maybe we could leave an anonymous tip about his location. I'm sure the deputy will start a search for him soon enough."

He hated sounding heartless, but given the circumstances, leaving Cold Springs as soon as possible was the only thing on his mind.

"I understand," Cassie quietly said. She ran her fingers through her hair, fiddling with the ends as if to distract herself. "And you promise you can help me? I have one more night to transform, and I'm scared of what I might do."

Liam wasn't entirely prepared for Cassie to transform one more night. He figured he'd be on the road, heading back to Blood Moon with a tied-up stranger.

"I'll figure something out, but until then, we need to be clear on a story in case the deputy asks us anything."

"Why would he?"

Liam accelerated. "I saw him with Peter. I don't know if Peter said anything, but I want to be prepared."

Cassie looked out the window. "Well, that's easy," she said, her blue eyes meeting his for a moment. "You were with me." She took a long pause before shrugging. "The whole night."

With a track record of taking things out of context, Liam understood clearly what Cassie was implying.

"That would be a reasonable alibi," he said, clearing his throat to hide his embarrassment.

"It's going to have to do, unless you can come up with something else?"

"Nope, that will work."

Cassie's shoulders relaxed. "Once we're in town, take a right. My apartment is just beyond the cemetery. I've got a comfy couch, though I doubt either of us will be able to sleep. I have so many questions."

"I know," Liam responded as he accelerated.

The wheels hugged a curve as Liam made his way back into town, passing the old barn with the words Welcome to Cold Springs.

EPILOGUE

eter Adams lay in a broken state, his blood barely pulsing through his veins as his pale skin reflected white in the moonlight. The young man with a promising future was now changed forever.

Though his body was damaged, his vital organs were still intact, allowing a fate worse than death to move within his weak body. The unforgiving virus—the affliction, the curse—which coursed through Cassie's veins and lingered in her saliva, moved through his bloodstream, attacking his immune system, assimilating his protective cells, and producing millions more within minutes.

Like a horde of mindless drones, the infected cells began the month-long process of reconstructing his body to the point of transformation. The affliction began on the molecular level, correcting the DNA anomalies that would impede the virus from spreading. It moved to the organs, perfecting their functions, and sealed any superficial wounds while stimulating the process of producing more blood at a rapid rate. Gradually, the color returned to Peter's skin as fresh blood pumped through his weak heart.

Peter's fingers and toes twitched. His gash slowly began to seal. Within the horrifying light of the moon, as the virus revived his basic bodily functions in order to prepare for the upcoming weeks of his supernatural transformation, Peter's lips parted and he took a gulp of air.

Living within the western shadow of the Rocky Mountains, M. E. Hansen is a cross genre author and lover of all things supernatural and romantic. When she's not getting excited about the next plot twist in her latest book, she's running a house full of monkeys, taming a vicious Norwegian Forest cat, and falling endlessly in love with her ingenious do-gooder of a husband.

You can follow M. E. Hansen on Instagram: @Author_MEHansen

Or visit her website at: www.authormehansen.com

A lastly, what did you think about The Cold Springs Killer? Leave a review on Amazon or Goodreads and tell others all about it. What did you like? What did you hate? Were the characters engaging? Was the suspense . . . suspenseful? Did you see Cassie's reveal coming a mile away? Your honest review will help other readers decide on whether to take a road trip to Cold Springs in search of The Cold Springs Killer.

I observe the full moon, recalling the extreme measures Henry has taken to keep himself in good standing with society. I might accept that economically my union to Selene would be frowned upon, but the thought of societal pressure forcing her to marry Jerome fills me with a deep pain. If she marries another, the only consolation I could hope for is her happiness, but she would be miserable with him.

"Where are we?" Keagan asks, interrupting my self-loathing.

I turn my gaze to the surrounding trees and the path

we stand upon. I shrug and decide to continue following the path, curious of where it leads. Keagan reluctantly follows, letting out a tired sigh. We push through a few more walls of willow until we come to an open space unlike anything I've ever seen.

Tall stone pillars align evenly in a large circle, moss clinging to their weathered sides and filling in large cracks. I step from the path and onto freshly cut grass, the clippings brushed to the base of each stone. I carefully walk to the nearest column, observing flecks of silver reflecting the moon's light. There are seven pillars total, each varying in height but still towering over Keagan and me. Some are eroded to slanted points, while others are cracked and falling apart. Surrounding the circle of stones is a dense forest. Rays of moonlight break up the darkness, accentuating silhouettes of tree trunks and craggily branches. A misty fog blankets the fauna as crickets chirp in the distance.

"What is this place?" Keagan asks, his voice a low whisper.

I shrug. Selene has never allowed our long walks to go beyond the topiary. "I don't know. Perhaps ruins of an ancient castle."

I find a stone altar placed between two of the pillars

to our right. It's made of a darker stone and stands about the height of a table. Behind the altar, moss covered steps glisten in the moon's light. Another set of steps are further north, blanketed in shadow by surrounding oak trees.

I inspect the altar, my mind racing now. Could this have been the place Henry killed the witch? Is his hidden cellar nearby?

My questions are interrupted by a low growl coming from the forest.

"What was that?" Keagan asks, searching the surrounding shadows. "I don't recall the Addingtons having any hounds."

The growl comes again, calling my attention to the trees behind one of the pillars. Carefully I step to Keagan's side, seeing the terrified look on his face.

Within the shadows something crouches close to the ground. At first I think it's a small animal startled by our presence and warning us to keep our distance. But then the creature stands upon two thick legs, rising to practically the height of a doorway.

I catch my breath, and my knees lock.

The beast's long arms reach to its knees, and its body rises and falls with each exhale. It remains still, hidden in the shadows, but is clearly making its presence known.

"Should we run?" Keagan asks, his voice still quiet but shrill.

I keep a close observation on the creature, wondering what it is. My pulse quickens and the hairs on the back of my neck prickle. Its eyes remind me of a man's, circular and encompassing. But the most disturbing thing about them, the most unnatural characteristic, is the glowing red color against the void of shadow.

A snarl escapes the figure, more aggressive now, causing Keagan and I to quake.

"Devin," Keagan says nervously, "what is that thing?"

I swallow hard, remembering where I've seen those eyes, sinewy limbs, and pointed black ears. I gawk at the sharp teeth and long snout. I'd locked the image away in the back of my mind, shrouded in myth and whispers.

"It's not a thing, exactly, but who," I reply.

Keagan shoots me an acidic look. "What are you talking about?"

I take one last deep breath, steadying my racing heart. "It's Henry Addington."

I stare at the monster, my legs as heavy as lead. I've faced danger before, life threatening even, but I've never seen such a creature, and I'm not sure how to react.

"Henry Addington?" Keagan repeats. Squinting his eyes, he takes a lingering look. "You mean the deranged man who murdered his sons two-hundred years ago?" Keagan returns his gaze to the red-eyed shadow and instinctively steps back. "You're mad."

Still within the shadows, the beast growls again, prompting me to slowly back away. "It's Henry Addington, cursed to punish those who aren't worthy of the Addingtons' social circle. The old woman was right. Man beasts are real."

BOOM!

The sky fills with flickering red and white light.

The fireworks scream into the dark sky, competing with the moon's light and announcing their end with a thunderous boom.

I return my gaze to the forest, finding the monster gone.

More fireworks burst, blanketing the trees in red light.

Keagan's chest heaves. "I don't like this one bit. Perhaps we should run," he says, his voice shaky and shrill.

ACKNOWLEDGEMENTS

This is the part of the book that readers aren't required to read, but if you wish to take a little behind the scenes stroll with me, you are more than welcome.

The idea for this book started with a simple thought out of the blue. I had recently published my first novel *Whispers of Addington Manor* September of 2021, and was preparing for my next project which I would start working on that following October. With the time in between projects, I remember wanting to maintain a schedule of writing each day and chose to work on writing prompts or free write projects. This is where the idea struck me to create a template from my favorite 90s TV sitcom and write a short story from the template I created. I never intended to publish the outcome of such a thought, but followed through, selecting a children's animated TV episode, and watching it scene for scene.

I broke down the vital components of each scene like I would an outline. Once finished, I modified the template to a story quite different from the original medium.

The first draft was an eight-chapter story about a widower tracking a murderer. There wasn't much else to it, besides the double plot twists at the end. I followed my template (plot outline) and wrote each chapter in one day, taking little time to draft out my story.

Then I shelved it.

I had another project I wanted to work on. October came and went, along with November and with the passing months I realized the next project I was working on wasn't going as smoothly as I had planned. So I took a break for December and decided to return to Cold Springs and continue on with Liam's journey.

By my second draft, I added two additional chapters and one additional character. I tried to flesh out my characters and detail the scenes that would set the tone for the story. Originally Matthew Larsen was the plucky character that desired to prove monsters were real and brushed aside his traumatic feelings to focus on attaining his proof. Matthew gave the story a campy feel, but I didn't mind it because it was reminiscent of the TV show I based the template on. After reading over it one last time, I was ready to move on.

By draft three, I enlisted the logical observations of my beloved husband. Though not a professional editor, he could spot a plot hole a mile away, or detect an underdeveloped character, or situation that just doesn't make sense. He provided tough love comments that inspired me to work a little harder in making the story the best it could be. He also prepared me for the real editor and how to handle any feedback I may struggle with. After making the necessary revisions from his red pencil marks, I contacted my Beta Readers.

Draft four is always a crucial draft because of the additional eyes that read over the project. I contacted a number of friends and family, hoping they'd be interested in reading a contemporary short story and provide feedback of their first impressions and thoughts. This stage usually begins the increased stress levels as I'm always nervous about their feedback, no matter what they say. I see this stage as an opportunity for growth as a writer and improving the story. Beta readers also help catch important or missing details of the plot I may not have seen. I'm so grateful for their feedback and words of encouragement. Though many wished to remain unnamed, I wanted to thank each of them, knowing that I couldn't have accomplished this thrilling tale without their thoughts, nit-pickiness, and questions. Two particular readers I wanted to say thanks to was Cristina and Jaime. Their willingness to read my strange stories means the world to me and their comments always help build my characters and realism. Another anonymous beta reader I wanted to thank, helped tremendously with their words of encouragement. I don't think my struggle with perfectionism will ever go away, but I took to heart the positive comments and helpful compliments along with the observations of a tender reader who I will always admire.

The feedback I received from all my sweet beta readers was incredibly helpful and surprisingly shifted the direction and tone of this story because of their insights.

I wanted to mention how important the Beta Reading stage of the process is because a particular beta reader mentioned how traumatized Matthew Larsen would be if I tried to base this story as close to reality as possible. I remember taking a moment to think about their comment. I agreed with the acknowledgement of how chipper Matthew was and how terrified he should have been instead. I know I wouldn't want to go camping, let alone a walk, in the forest if ever I encountered such a terrifying situation. And so I decided to switch him out with a different character. But there weren't any other characters that survived, until I remember that there was: Peter Adams.

When switching Matthew to Peter the whole tone of the book changed dramatically.

For months I made the necessary revisions from the beta feedback as well as adjusting the story to match Peter's encounter and how that would affect the plot. Though I kept true to the concept of the story, a widower tracking that crazy killer, there was something more added when I focused on Peter. The conversation in the diner helped shape what kind of theme the story would take on. His character wanted revenge and felt killing a killer was the best option, but Peter didn't understand what kind of company he was dealing with. I maintained my unreliable narration as long as I could, alluding that Liam wanted the same thing as Peter. Let's just say, I was satisfied with the outcome of subverting most of my beta reader's expectations when they got to chapter 9 and chapter 10.

It was also during this stage where I learned the significance of taking a sense of pride in my work. I had an interaction with one of my readers who gave critical feedback, the kind that made me question what kind of story I'm writing. At first, I downplayed my project, comparing it to a campy b-movie. I wasn't entirely proud of the story nor my writing, but I didn't hate it. But as I made excuses for the things the story lacked; I realized I wasn't truly giving it my all when it came to writing.

This troubled me. For years I'd wanted to write stories and share the goings-ons in my head. I expected to be working on a different project, one that mattered more, that had a deeper meaning to myself as a mother, a book that I was passionate about. But instead, I was working a story that didn't mean as much at the time and was turning into a hurried experience just to get onto the next great project. But as I looked over the feedback, the suggestions, the questions, and how Peter's storyline would change so much of the story, I decided to dedicate as much seriousness to this manuscript as I would to any other passion project. I took the time to think, to learn, to improve. And though it still may not be the kind of story I really wanted to tell, *The Cold Springs Killer* has definitely left its mark on me, not only as a writer, but as a person.

When I was finally satisfied with my revisions, I read

over the story one more time. For any aspiring writers reading this, remember to love the manuscript you're working on because you will either become the books number one fan, or its harshest critic for how many times you'll go over it.

Then came the Editor stage.

Working with an editor can be a special experience. For me, it's always helpful. I remember while working on *Whispers* I was hesitant to get a professional editor to look over my work, but I knew if I wanted to improve, I needed the extra help. Working on this book was no different. I'm so grateful for my editor's amazing abilities in capturing what it takes to create a great story and to understand where I'm going with it.

She helped me understand the importance of sticking to one character's point of view at a time. This proved helpful when trying to keep Cassie's secret under wraps. Thank you, Angela, for your help.

After everything was finalized with edits and final revisions, it was time to format and publish.

I acknowledge the process of writing this particular book because it wasn't a single-handed experience. This story started out as a writing exercise and became so much more.

Thank you to all who helped and supported the making of this book. The simplest things can make a world of difference in somebody else's life, and I'm proof of that.

--M. E. Hansen